Scanning, uploading and/or distribution of this book via the Internet, print, audio recordings or any other means, without the written permission of the Publisher is illegal and will be prosecuted to the fullest extent of the law.

Except for select brand names and businesses, this book is a work of fiction. Names, places, events and characters are fictitious. Any similarities to actual events or persons, living or dead, are purely coincidental.

CYNICAL PLAY

L. M. Causey

Illustrations by Winnchester

© 2024

ISBN : 978-1-946766-81-6

All rights reserved. Except for review purposes, the reproduction of this book in whole or part, electronically or mechanically, constitutes a copyright violation.

Published by Romance Divine LLC

DEDICATION

To my parents and Ken.
THANK YOU!

FROM the AUTHOR

"Some think jackaling is a cynical play
and if you end up in the bin, it is.

If you don't, then it's play on."

L.M. Causey

The ISLAND

CHAPTER 1

4 months later…

I'm awakened by someone yelling my name. I'm still mostly asleep, but I know it's Jack. I hit the light on the bedside table as Jack forces his way through the door. "What the hell, Jack?"

He's grabbing random clothes from the closet and throwing them at me. "Get up! We've got to get to your island."

I don't question him; I make quick work of getting my clothes on. I dart into the bathroom to put my contacts in. "Jack?" I yell.

He appears in the doorway. "The emergency alarms were triggered, and we can't get any of our men on their radios. According to Eric, you told him the island was in use." I look at him and finally realize exactly what he's saying, and I know it's showing on my face. I pull on my boots, grab my phone and check for messages. There are none and the emptiness on the screen sinks in my gut like a boulder. I run through the living room to grab my to-go bag off the couch as we head to the elevators. I can hear Jack's boots right behind me. I also know he's on the phone confirming our plane is ready to go.

I hit speed dial on my phone and call the only person I know who can help us. "Tiny, it's me, get to the island as fast as you can. Take all the men you can find. The alarms have gone off and he's there alone. Find him, Tiny." I hang up and kick the elevator wall hard enough to leave a dent. I bend over trying not to scream or throw up as I close my eyes.

"Alex, what's he doing there alone?" Jack's question knocks the air right out of me.

"He was rehabbing an injury and contemplating retirement," I say to my reflection in the polished steel of the elevator door.

Jack keeps pushing the button on the panel as if it will make it move faster. I know he needs to do something other than stand still. The doors open and an SUV is already running with the doors open. I jump in, toss my bag on the floor, and slam the door. Jack gets in and the driver puts the SUV in gear. He leaves a layer of rubber on the garage floor as we are forced back into our seats.

It's three in the morning so traffic to the private airport is thin and my driver isn't obeying many of the traffic laws. I feel a hand on my shoulder, and I whip around in my chair to find Cane sitting behind me in his usual spot. I stare over at Jack and if looks could kill, Jack would have been vaporized. "Cane, what the fuck are you doing? You're not needed on this trip. You can go back with the SUV."

Cane's voice is calm, "Jack thought you might need someone with my skill set, but if you want me to stay here, I will."

We pulled up to the airport, our driver honking the horn as security opens the gates without delay. The plane is already running, and our driver unlocks the SUV doors while the vehicle is still moving.

We are out, with boots on the ground, before the SUV comes to a full stop. As I make my way up the stairs, I see Cane standing next to the SUV. I shake my head and yell at him, "Something has gone horribly wrong, and Jack might be right, your skill set may in fact be useful. Get on the damn plane."

I get on the plane and tell the pilot to get us off the ground as soon as possible. I take my seat without putting anything away. Cane and Jack choose seats as far away from me as they can get. It takes less than fifteen minutes for the pilot to get us cleared and off the ground. The lone flight attendant lets me know I can turn on my laptop. All three of us get out our various devices and get to work.

I'm trying to reach Tiny to see how close he and his people are. Jack is trying to find any team we may have worked with who might be even vaguely close to the island. Cane is coordinating with Kenzie on anything we may need regarding tech support. It will take about ten hours for us to get to the island and I know Tiny will get there in half the time. Either way, by the time anyone gets there, whatever is going on will be over. I would like to hope this is the hardest part, but I know damn well, it won't be.

I finally reach Tiny, and he tells me they are making good time. He also lets me know he has called everyone and anyone he knows who may be able to get to the island faster than he can. I know he has family on the outlying islands, so there's a chance they can be there before he arrives. He tells me as soon as he knows something he'll contact me.

I'm getting constant notes from the pilot via the flight attendant. She clearly knows something is wrong. She's also been with us long enough to wait until she's needed and to stay out of the way otherwise. At the four and half hour mark the computer chimes. I know it's Tiny and I know he's arrived at the island. I also have a horrible feeling I don't want to hear what he's going to tell me.

"Tiny?" Is really all I can say when I see his face appear on my screen. Neither Jack nor Cane got out of their seat.

"I'm here; there's a mess Alex and it isn't good. We will secure the island and assess the situation. Anyone moving will be cared for. You can make any decisions when you get here. I'm with him and I'll stay with him until you arrive."

I take a deep breath. "Thank you."

Tiny nods and our call is disconnected.

I pick up the empty green glass water bottle in front of me and hurl it across the cabin. It smashes into pieces and the only person who moves is the flight attendant. This is not the first time she's had to clean up after me. I pull my blanket up over my head and try to sleep. I can hear Cane and Jack get out of their seats, and I hear them loading weapons. In a strange way these sounds give me great comfort.

When the captain announces we are forty-five minutes from landing, I get up and make my way to the bathroom to brush my teeth and put drops in my eyes. I straighten myself up and put on the bravest face I can manage. I get back to my seat to find my leg holster, my H&K, and two additional clips laying in it. Alongside, is my large knife in a sheath I can attach to my belt once on the ground.

Jack and Cane take turns in the restroom. The captain lets us know we are on approach. We take our seats, and the landing gear goes down. As soon as we touch down Jack is up and waiting by the door for the plane to come to a complete stop. We are stopped for only a few minutes when we hear the knock from the other side. Jack makes quick work of the door; I'm already standing behind him and Cane is standing quietly behind me.

We are down the steps and into the waiting SUVs in a matter of seconds. The group of SUV's speed across the island and come to a screeching halt next to the dock. We're out of the vehicles and into the speed boat in record time. I recognize one of Tiny's many cousins at the wheel, he simply nods hello. We brace ourselves as he pushes down the throttle. We reach the island, where the compound is, in record time. Tiny's cousin slows and I'm about to yell at him to keep going when I see why he has brought us up short. There are bodies in the water. They're our men and they've been tied to buoys. There is also debris surrounding them, which I surmise are the boats they were in.

When we finally reach the beach, I don't wait for the boat to be pulled further onto the sand. I jump out and the water is up to my calves. The freezing water brings on a harsh wave of reality. I get to the beach and one of

CYNICAL PLAY

Tiny's men points to the main house and puts up two fingers. This tells me Tiny is on the second floor. I turn and look at Jack and he nods in acknowledgement. He grabs Cane's arm and says something to him. They both start talking to Tiny's men, and I head into the house. I can vaguely hear Jack giving instructions about gathering evidence and collecting the dead.

I can see from the bodies heading up the stairs our team gave as good as they got, and I know from their sacrifice we will be able to find out who did this. I call out to Tiny as I reach the top of the stairs. Not to tell him I'm there, but to ensure he won't shoot me.

"I'm in your room, cousin." I take a deep breath despite the smell and walk into the room. I immediately saw him lying on the floor. Based on the destruction in the room, he put up a fight, this was never in doubt. For several long moments I only see him in the room. When I finally look up at Tiny, I motion wordlessly with my hand encompassing the room as I realize there should be more people in here. He knows the question I'm asking.

"I threw the fuckers who killed him, out the window. I didn't want the assholes spirits mingling with his. I wanted you to be able to be alone with him when you got here." I know my eyes are filling with tears, so I nod in appreciation. Before the first tear falls, Tiny leaves the room without a sound and closes the door behind him.

I notice the room is freezing. Tiny must have turned the air conditioning on high when he arrived. I get a clean sheet from the closet and cover him. I fold the sheet back to his chest and sit down next to him. I know it's not him, not really. I hope a part of him is still here with me. I hope he waited for me to get here. I need to apologize, and I need to say goodbye. Death is not about the dead but more about the regrets of the living. He was considerate in life, and I must believe he would be the same in death. I don't know how long I'd been sitting there when I heard a light knock on the door.

"What?" I croak out softly even though it sounds loud in the empty room.

I hear Jack's voice through the door. "Is it okay if we clean out the house?"

I put some strength in my voice, "Yes."

I hear another knock and know it's Jack's confirmation. There's noise outside the room for a while and then there is quiet again.

I can hear a prayer song coming through the open window getting louder and closer. This tells me Tiny, and his men have completed the litter to take his body down to one of the boats so he can go home. His second passion was helicopters and gliders. We'll tell his family he died in a crash, and no one will say any different.

I have said everything I wanted and needed to say. I say my final goodbye, stand up and open the door. Tiny is standing there with three other men equal in size. They come into the room and gently place him, sheet and all, onto the litter. Tiny takes the lead, and they lift the body. I follow behind them down the stairs. They continue to sing the prayer as we make our way out of the house.

When the front door opens there are no human sounds except for singing. The men have all stopped working and the dead have been moved. There's a large yacht waiting off the beach. Tiny and his men will take his body out to it and take him home. I can see Jack and Cane standing in line with the other men. We reach the small boat which will take them out to the yacht. I lift the sheet over his left arm. There I find the bracelet he only wore when he was on the island. I slide it off his wrist and lean down and kiss his forehead and whisper, "No worries." Silently, I promise him I'll find every person who knew about this, every person who had a hand in it, the one who gave the order, and all will suffer in ways not even imagined in hell. I slide the bracelet on to my wrist and up my forearm until it fits. I cover him with the sheet and place my hand on his chest as I walk with the men into the water so his body can be loaded on to the boat. Once they have him secured, I say goodbye to Tiny and his men. They leave slowly without another word.

The singing on the island stopped and I turned to find myself standing alone on the shore. I go back to the house and collect the few things I want. When I start to head down the stairs Cane is standing at the bottom. He reaches out and I give him the box. I make my way to the porch and stand looking out at the beach. I hear boots behind me. I turn and Jack is standing there smoking. Before today I would have hurt him for smoking in this house, but now Jack knows it doesn't matter. I walk away from the house towards the beach.

Jack walks a few paces behind briefing me. "All of our people have been collected. Two are still alive, but only because the chilly water helped to slow the blood loss. Also, Tiny's men managed to find two of the intruders alive. They will be turned over to the interrogation team I managed to get a hold of."

I nod, mostly so he knows I'm listening. There are additional boats waiting at the shoreline, with men I vaguely recognize, all waiting for instructions.

Cane walks up to me, "Who would you like me to travel with?" I look at him and see he wants only an answer, nothing more.

"Go with the boat meeting the interrogators and get me some damn actionable intel." He turns to head for the appropriate boat. I turn and look back at the house and feel a hand on my shoulder, and I know it's Cane. As soon as the hand was there it's gone. I hear the distant sounds of a plane taking off. This tells me our men are being transported to the nearest medical center which might be able to save them.

"What do you want to do?" Jack asks between exhales.

I look around and feel the rage wash over me. "Burn it to the ground. Burn the whole fucking thing to the ground. Then I want it blown up and sunk to the bottom of the fucking ocean." Jack nods and makes his way over to the rest of Tiny's men and gives them instructions.

I'm not really paying attention to how long I've been standing there. I can vaguely feel the water pushing up over my boots. I notice there's an open hand in front of me and in it is a lighter. I reached out for the lighter and turned to see Jack standing there smoking away.

"Everything is set up. Walk around and light the marks. I sent Tiny's men home with cash. We can send a wire when we get back. Cane is with the interrogation team, and I'll be out on the other large boat. Tiny already left."

CYNICAL PLAY

I nod and walk away from Jack without saying anything. As I began to light all the red and black markers Jack left for me, parts of the island start to burn.

There's a large pile of bodies at the opposite end away from the house, covered by palm leaves; there are markers around the pile, and I light those as well. I know they are only the bad guys, since we would never leave our guys in a dump with the fuckers who killed them. We always return our dead to their families. I got back to where I started and turned to see the palm trees and house engulfed in flames.

There's a boat waiting for me with Tiny's son at the wheel.

"Can we go out a bit so I can finish watching it burn?" I ask and he nods.

I get in and he slowly backs us out onto the ocean. He takes us out far enough so if one of the palms fall it won't hit us. I sit and watch.

What was once the best place I had ever been is turning into a pile of ash. When there are no lights coming from the island, I ask him to take me to wherever they took the old guy. We pull alongside a yacht the size of a small city block. I walk up the gangway and find Jack sitting on the deck smoking and drinking a beer. He has a tablet up on the table in front of him. I look over his shoulder and can hear Cane's voice.

I quickly understand he has a live feed of the interrogation. I reach into the fridge behind Jack's chair and grab water. I take a seat and motion for him to turn it up. Cane is standing before one of the men and for reasons unknown he has removed his shirt. I point and look at Jack.

"I think they may have turned the heat up for the interrogation, or he may have gotten pieces of the asshat on his shirt. I vote it's the latter." I put my feet up on one of the other chairs and watch as Cane extracts every bad deed this guy has ever done and for who.

When I have seen enough, I pat Jack on the shoulder. I lay down on one of the lounge chairs on the giant deck, "Remind me to give Cane a raise when this is over." The screams from Cane's interrogation are the last things I hear before I drift off to sleep.

CHAPTER 2

I wake with the sunrise. Jack decided to leave me on deck and was nice enough to cover me with a blanket. I'm going to need to see the acupuncturist and chiropractor after this. Lounge chairs are not meant to be slept on overnight. I slowly make my way into the main cabin in search of a bathroom. I found a nice state room with an en-suite. On the bed are clothes in my size and next to those a small plastic case with bathroom essentials. On top of the clothes lay a note. "Jacob said these would work for you," signed 'G' .

    I make my way into the bathroom and do my best to try to clean the remnants of yesterday off me. I spend a good portion of the shower sitting on the bench letting the water wash over me. Unfortunately, it also included a good amount of screaming and crying. When I pulled my shit together, I emerged from the bathroom and my old clothes were gone. I dressed in clean clothes and noticed at the foot of the bed are all black cross-trainers. They are my size, so I put them on and left the room to look for Jack.

    I find him sitting in a large room, which is used as a board room, however, it was currently set up with a breakfast buffet. "Did you ask for all this food?"

    "Nope," Jack tossed a piece of kiwi into his mouth, "it was here when I walked in."

CYNICAL PLAY

I raise my eyebrow at him, but he continues eating. I hear the door to my right open and a young man enters the room with a tray of tea. He motions with his head for me to take a seat.

I take a seat across from Jack and the young man places the tea down in front of me. The tray has a wide selection of both loose and bagged tea along with four to five kinds of honey. I look up at him and he winks. Jacob must have been on the phone since we left to make sure this was all in place.

I mix my tea and look out at the ocean. I realize part of my problem is I don't know where to start from all the chaos we discovered on the island. As I'm about to say something to Jack, one of the doors to the deck slides opens, Cane walks in. He has clearly been swimming. I'm not sure if him being here is a good or bad sign.

Cane puts his towel over a chair and pulls the shirt he has in his hand over his head. He walks around the table and takes a seat next to Jack.

Jack gives Cane a nod, "I take it since you were swimming this morning, you got what we needed out of those two pieces of shit last night?"

Cane replies in an even tone. "There's nothing those pieces of shit have done, and no one they have worked for, we don't know about. I passed all the information to Kenzie, and he should be ready any time to brief you on the specifics. I was using the ocean to wash up. It seemed easier to let it all float away with the salt, rather than waste the ships' water. I was a bit of a mess when I arrived."

I look at him, really look at him, and see his knuckles are a bit of a mess. Also, there is swelling around his left eye and staples at his hair line near his left temple.

Jack also takes in his appearance and asks him, "Did you slip and fall or something? The last time I checked the video you were talking to a guy tied to a chair with trailer strapping."

Cane touches his eye, thinking. "The guy in the chair was the first one. He took only a little bit of persuasion to start talking. I had to get creative with the second guy. He was reluctant to share what he knew. He thought he could hold back information in the hope we would see him as more useful alive. I convinced him otherwise."

I nodded and continued to drink my tea. I can hear a phone ringing. Jack pulls my phone out of his shirt pocket, looks at the caller's I.D. and slides it across the polished wood table to me. I stop it with my hand and look at the screen; it's Tiny. I slide my finger across the screen and put the phone up to my ear. Tiny tells me everything's taken care of, and he hangs up. I let his words set in, then slid the phone back to Jack and turned to look out the giant picture windows behind me.

Jack asks Cane to check with Kenzie, once he has eaten, to see how far away we are from our first target. I hear, what I assume is Cane's chair slide on the floor followed by a sliding door opening and closing.

Jack knocks on the table and says in a muffled voice, "I guess he wasn't hungry."

I rise from my chair and walk past Jack. He raises his hand as I walk by, and I grab it for a moment as I pass. Jack passes me a memory stick. I put it in my pocket as I leave out the side door making my way to the highest deck. I stayed up there for a while, with my thoughts and the ocean as my only company. A nice young man keeps bringing me water and at one point, he opens an umbrella over me.

Jack interrupts my silence with one of his damn stadium whistles. I smile briefly to myself. I know Jack didn't want to look all over this floating palace so he figures if he whistles long and loud enough, I will eventually appear. I collected myself and went looking for him, finding both he and Cane on the main deck under umbrellas with three 40-inch TVs in front of them. Cane has a computer hooked up and running. Jack looks up and sees me standing there. He pulls a chair out for me so I can see the TV screens.

He's the first to speak. "Kenzie has information for us we can act on from where we are. I thought you'd like to hear it firsthand."

I nod and concentrate on the screens.

Cane taps on the keyboard and Kenzie appears on one of the screens. "Hey brother, it's good to see you. Is the boss, ok?" I look up at Jack with an eyebrow raised. Jack points at the single camera on the table and I realize Kenzie can only see Cane. I nod and sit further back in the chair.

"Brother, the boss is fine and can hear you. The old goat is here too, but it's questionable if he can hear you."

I hear Kenzie laugh and I can't help but smile.

Jack moves past the comment, "Kenzie, what did you find?"

"Well, so far, we have been able to verify, from those guys you chatted with, that what they told you is true. The good news is they don't seem to have compartmentalized their operation, if they did, we happened on at least one of the guys who knew most, if not all, of the moving parts."

Cane asks, "Kenzie, can you share your screen? I have additional screens set up here so we can see what you have. Remember Jack needs large print."

"Keep it up kid and I'm going to feed you to the sharks." Jack snarks back shoving Cane's shoulder.

I shake my head and watch the screens as they begin to fill with information and photos. A face appears on the screen, and I lean forward and tap on the screen.

"Hold up Kenzie, the boss has spotted something." Cane says.

I keep tapping the screen and Jack reads aloud the number on the bottom of the photo.

"Got it." Kenzie says, and Cane moves the photo to the screen closest to me and enlarges the photo. The related information begins to appear on the middle screen. I begin to read the background Kenzie has put together. I can see this guy is a major player and has his hand in a bunch of pies. I can't say I have ever heard his name, Thomas Wright. Of course, it may not be his real name, but there is something familiar about his face. "Get me a family tree on this guy," is all I say as I get up and make my way back indoors.

I can see Jack and Cane still talking to Kenzie as I sit at the giant table, where the food was available earlier. The same young man brings me more tea and quietly leaves the room without a word.

CYNICAL PLAY

As the sun begins to set, Jack and Cane join me. Jack drops a notepad in front of me.

"Kenzie is putting together a file, but these are the highlights."

I skim down the page looking for anything which rings a bell. I see it and it didn't hurt Jack has circled it in red about a hundred times. Our target is JD Kranston, older brother of Jim Lee Kranston, our former employee. The same Jim Lee Kranston who became fertilizer last year after violating our policy of fornicating with a co-worker.

As I sit there and stare at the name all I can think of is my decision cost one of the best people I ever knew, his life. There are things you never fully recover from, and this will be a constant pain for me.

I tap my finger on the pad and look over at Jack with a question on my face.

"It appears," Jack explains, "JD Kranston hasn't had any real contact with Jim Lee in years. However, the father had been beating the drum since his death. The father died of natural causes four months ago and now the brother has taken over his business and subsequently the search to find out what happened to his little brother."

I lean forward with my elbows on the table. I clasp my hands together and rest my head on them. I'm trying to control my rage so I can make the correct decision. "How insulated is he?"

"From what Kenzie could find he keeps a tight inner circle. He has on hand security, and he changes residences every three to five weeks. Kenzie is still looking for a pattern in how he chooses where to stay and when."

I exhale a deep breath and stare down at the paper. I look over at Cane. "Does he have any other family members?"

"Yes, he has a wife and a couple of kids. He stops in to see them only when his presence is required. They appear to live far outside the other parts of his life. He does have an older son from his younger days. He's twenty something and it looks like he's part of his father's business. The father and son have two to three girls each on the side."

I begin to click my thumb nail between my teeth as the thoughts rush through my head. "We don't kill young children, and unless the wife knows something or gets in the way, we leave them all alone. Check on the girlfriends. If they are part of his enterprise I want to know. Ironically, his son may be the way in."

Jack takes out his phone and calls Kenzie, putting him on speaker. "Kenzie, we need a full rundown on the bastard son, and we need to know what his current location is. Also look at their side pieces. We need to know if they're involved in the business in any way."

I can hear Kenzie pounding away on the keys and talking to himself as he does it.

Kenzie's voice comes over the speaker. "Ok, it looks like the kid is on vacation and spending like a demon on one of the corporate cards. It looks like he is currently located… fuck!"

Cane leans in, "Kenzie what is it?"

"This stupid fucker is here. He's in Las Vegas!" Kenzie replies with disgust.

I look up at Jack. "I want him in custody as soon as humanly possible." I turn to Cane, "Get us the hell out of here. I want to be the first person this fuck sees when the hood comes off."

Cane nods and makes a beeline to find the captain. We need to get someplace where we can get back to our plane and ultimately back to Las Vegas.

Jack takes the phone off speaker and continues to talk to Kenzie. He tells him to give the computers back to the experts and get Teams 1 and 2 prepared to meet us. There's further discussions and logistical issues discussed before Jack hangs up. I'm not paying attention to any details. I know Jack will inform me where I need to be when the time comes.

Once Jack ends the call, he sits down in the chair next to me. I'm staring out at the ocean again. "I'm going to do horrible things to these people. I do need to decide if I'm going to send this idiot back to his dear father whole or a piece at a time."

Jack's simple reply is, "I vote for pieces."

Cane comes back and tells us it will be two hours until we get to a private air strip where our plane can pick us up.

"Cane, can I use the laptop you had?"

Cane disappears down the hallway and returns with the computer. He sets it down in front of me. I take the memory stick out of my pocket. I pushed it into the side of the laptop, and as suspected, it's the interrogation footage.

"Cane how far into this do you get the information on Kranston's brother?"

"It's at the end of the second guy's chat. I would say about ten or fifteen minutes before the end."

I scroll to the end of the footage and watch as Cane delivers a cracking blow to the guy's right shoulder. The sound of the bones breaking is as loud as the screaming. The guy drops to his knees both arms hanging limp at his side. There's blood splattered on the walls and the ceiling. I would bet it belongs to the guy on his knees but from the look of it, Cane also contributed. I watch Cane push his thumbs into both shoulder joints and extract the name we have since confirmed is the alias. Thomas Wright and Jim Lee's brother, JD Kranston, are one in the same.

Cane is standing before him and the man is screaming and sobbing, "I swear to everything holy; I have told you all I know."

Cane calmly kneels in front of him, so they are face to face. He places his hand over the man's nose and mouth. The man's eyes widened from surprise and the lack of oxygen.

Without saying a word Cane continues to hold his hand over the man's nose and mouth until he suffocates. I have to say his death brings me considerable comfort.

I close the laptop and push away from the table. I can feel tears welling in my eyes, and I'll be damned if I'll cry in front of an audience. I stop next to Cane's chair and he's kind enough not to look up at me. I put my hand on his shoulder. I walk back to my room and climb back into the shower to try to wash all the ugly memories away, again.

Cane looks up at Jack. "Is she going to recover from this?"

CYNICAL PLAY

Jack rubs both hands over his two-day beard and stands up. "Kid, as with anything this personal, it will take her time to accept she couldn't have prevented it. She's going to recover better knowing we are here and ready to do our job."

"Is there something I need to look out for?"

As Jack opens the door to go back to his room he turns to answer the question. "If she kills someone without getting information which gets us closer to the head of the snake you let me know. Until then, she can, and will do, whatever the hell she wants."

Cane nods, gets out of the chair, picks up the computer and heads back to the room he has chosen to use while on board.

I emerge from the shower and find clean clothes on the bed and the old ones have been taken away. I dress and sit on the edge of the bed. I'm sitting, not really thinking about anything, when there's a knock on the door.

"Yeah."

I hear Jack's voice on the other side. "Can I come in?"

"Sure"

"First, we are about twenty minutes from getting to the plane. Next, I think Cane should take the first shot at the brat when we get our hands on him. Lastly, I have spoken to Kenzie, and they have eyes on said brat as we speak. Also, the IT people have confirmed all the mistresses take no active part in JD or his son's business. One may know more than she should as she is a favorite of JDs, maybe some pillow talk, but she's not active in the organization. They purely support both men's extra-curricular activities."

I think about what Jack has said. I flop back on the bed and spread my arms out. "We should use a honey trap to get the brat. It'll be the easiest way to get him away from whatever babysitters he may have. I agree Cane should be the first one to interrogate him. However, I will be the first person the fucker sees when we take the hood off. Let me get my shoes on and I'll join you on deck."

Jack nudges my knee and leaves the room.

I feel the boat start to slow down as I get to my feet. I know there's no point in being ready for all this. It's better to get it done and move on to the next thing. As I head out to the main deck, I can see Jack and Cane are already there waiting.

We pull up to the dock and an SUV is waiting for us. Jack has our weapons with him, and he throws them in the back as he gets in. Cane is in front of me and opens the front passenger door. I get in and he shuts the door after me, taking his usual position behind me. As the SUV heads towards the landing strip, I take a moment to glance out at the ocean. You would think I would have more feelings about all of this, but for the moment everything is blank.

When we reach the plane, I take a seat in the rear while Jack and Cane take seats in the front. The flight attendant has already put out the food Jack likes. She was also nice enough to leave me my favorite seltzer water. Since Cane has not been with us for long, she asks him what he would like before takeoff.

CYNICAL PLAY

We all use the long flight to sleep without having to really worry about anything else. The flight attendant wakes us up about two hours out of Las Vegas. This gives us time to shower and change as needed. When we land in Las Vegas, Jack is the first one off the plane. I'm sure he's briefing the guys who have come to get us. Cane is waiting for me at the door. It's not so much I'm reluctant to start this, it's more I would prefer to end them all at once.

I take a deep breath and walk towards Cane. Once he sees me heading his way, he walks down the steps. I get to the steps and look out on two full teams of fifteen men standing shoulder to shoulder. Cane and Jack included. It's quite a sight. I can see each of them has a black arm band around their left upper arm. It's a very touching gesture. I'll have to remember to thank Kenzie when this is all done.

I reach the bottom step, and Cane breaks away to open the door to my waiting SUV. I pause before getting in and look back at the men. "Well, let's get moving, these cowardly mother fuckers aren't going to kill themselves," I say with all the piss and vinegar I can muster.

"Yes Ma'am!" is the rib rattling unison response I receive. The men all break off and get back into the SUV's.

I nod at Cane and take my seat as he shuts the door behind me. Kenzie's voice comes over the speaker system to tell us what's been put in motion since his last update.

CHAPTER 3

"Ok boss my team and I are at Mandalay Bay. We have six girls working on the casino floor. His tastes are random, so we figured we would give him more than one to choose from. I warned the girls this could get painful. They asked for payment of their medical bills and compensation for time away from work if anything happens. We have counted eight babysitters, and he always has two at his side. We also know he's staying in one of the residential suites at the top of the hotel. We've coordinated with the onsite security, and they were more than happy to find something else to do while we escort him from the property."

I wave my hand and Jack speaks up.

"Kenzie, we need the down and dirty, not so much on the specifics."

There is a pause before Kenzie speaks again. "Boss, I wanted to make sure you had all the information before going in."

I nod and Jack tells him to continue. Kenzie gives us the entire rundown and all the options he and his team produced.

"Boss, hold on my burner is ringing." We can hear bits and pieces of Kenzie's conversation. "Boss, he's invited two of our girls up to his room."

CYNICAL PLAY

I hear Cane laugh in the back seat. "Well, that seems a lot easier than I thought it would be," is all he says before I hear him check the clip in his weapon. Kenzie also tells us the hotel security has cleared the underground back of the house entrance for our arrival. Jack tells the driver to take us directly to the hotel.

Cane hands me my earwig and my H&K, I look at the weapon and hesitate. "If I see him now, I'll kill him, and it would defeat the purpose. So... I'll stay with the trucks and the ground crew." I turn to Jack, "You and Cane bring him down."

Cane looks at Jack and nods. Jack passes along the assignments over the radio. It's not long until we pull up to the VIP garage. Security opens the gate for us, and the SUV's pull in and turnaround so they're facing the exit. The guys exit the SUV's and make their way to the elevators. Security is holding the elevators for us, and they have the doors to the stairs propped open. Part of Kenzie's advance team is waiting with access cards to ensure the elevators don't stop until we want them to.

Jack nods and takes his position at the front. Cane taps his chest, and I can see a camera strapped to him. I tap my temple to acknowledge his good thinking, and he takes his position at the front, next to Jack.

The elevators close on the lead team and the other guys make their way up the stairwells. I look around to see who is still in the garage with me. I see a total of five have remained behind. There are three drivers who are also sharp shooters and two of the best hand-to-hand fighters we have. I have my weapon in my hand, at rest by my side, but it's more for them than for me. I can hear all the communication coming over my earwig. Kenzie gives the word and the security cameras along their routes are taken offline as they exit the elevator on the top floor.

Simultaneously Jack marks the elevator open as I hear suppressed and muffled gunfire over the earpiece. Jack lets us know a shot grazed Cane before the door guards were down. Kenzie had joined them from his overwatch spot in the stairwell utility closet. I start to roll my head stretching my neck.

My SUV driver shook his head, "Boss, don't you start with your crazy neck rollin' shit. Jack ain't here and nothin' good gonna come from gettin' mad down here."

I look at my driver and I know he is right. I concentrate on what is going on upstairs. I hear Kenzie say the elevator is clean. Which means he did a fast and dirty chemical drop to compromise any presumed future testing from being conclusive.

Cane is the next voice I hear. '"We have four down in the hallway, leaving four inside the suite."

I hear Jack give a three count before they breach the door. They enter the room with the pass key and there's a barrage of gunfire over the earpieces.

"One down." I hear Cane say.

I can hear women screaming. I can also hear an unfamiliar voice saying if our guys don't leave the room, he will order his men to kill the girls. Five of our best men are in the room and events unfold exactly as they were scripted. The two men at the rear fire on the women hitting them in the fleshy part of their outer thighs. As predicted, the women slump and become dead weight to the men holding them. They loosen their hold on the girls, and they crumple to the floor.

CYNICAL PLAY

Jack and Cane tap two shots through the center of the foreheads of the two men. Kenzie, as the center man, has his weapon focused on the man who remains in front of our target. I can hear two of our men in the stair well who have reached the top floor, and they quickly enter the room to carry the girls out.

A high-pitched voice starts yelling inside the room. "You have no idea what you've done! Me and my family are going to rain down the contents of Pandora's box on you fuckers!" I hear a voice tell the speaker to shut his mouth, but it's not a voice I recognize.

"Hey old man, do you think we should tell this ass hat we work for Pandora?"

I hear Jack laugh at Cane's question.

I left the monitor for Cane's chest camera on my seat but have yet to look at it. Instead preferring to listen to the events unfold. At this point I've heard enough and it's time I joined the party. I grab the radio out of the SUV. "Kenzie, make it so the room can hear me."

I hear a click and then Kenzie says, "Boss?"

"Good evening. I would appreciate it if you let my men take those two young women out of the room so they can get medical attention."

I wake up the tablet with a tap and I take this opportunity to get a look at our target. He's a ridiculous mass of useless muscle. It's all for show and I laugh a bit to myself.

The screechy voice brings me back to the situation as I bring my focus back to the tablet. "These whores are going to bleed out on this floor, and your assholes will go down for this." Again, I heard a voice tell him to shut his mouth. I realize it's his remaining bodyguard. Sadly, his common sense won't help either of them now.

I give the order. "Kenzie, whenever you're ready."

I hear a pop, and I see the red spray hit the back wall and the target, as the bodyguard crumples to the ground. The target is standing, muscles on full display, wearing only his suit pants. He has no weapon and no idea how to fight off Cane. He throws a haymaker but Cane steps to the side and brings his elbow down on the idiot's temple. The lump of a man crumples to the floor. Cane puts the hood over the target's head and pulls the drawstrings tight. He then trusses him up with zip-ties and heavy-duty towing rope. The women have been carried from the room and are first on the elevator so we can get them to our off-site medical facility.

Jack, Cane, and Kenzie all get into the second elevator. Cane and Jack are dragging our catch by the tow rope.

One of the SUV's loaded with the women and two of our best field medics exits quickly from the garage.

The rear of my SUV is open. Cane and Jack toss the target in the back and touch the auto shut button; we're not savages after all. The rest of the guys pour out of the stairwell and get into the remaining SUV's. Jack and Kenzie got into my SUV. Cane walks around to get in and I look at his arm. It looks to be a through and through. He nods and grabs my door until I get in. He shuts the door and gets in behind me and we exit the garage.

CYNICAL PLAY

We make it to our buildings in record time. Kenzie is the first one out of the SUV, his right-hand man Shaun is standing nearby with the transport cage he brought upstairs for our guest. He and Kenzie load our prisoner into it and get on the freight elevator to take him down to the detention level.

Despite Cane being shot, he gets out of the SUV before me and has my door open. I get out and wave to Jack who heads over to the weapons cage to drop off the equipment we took to the island. I'm standing face to face with Cane, and I'm having difficulty finding my words. Part of my brain sees him lying on the floor, blood everywhere, but I know it's not him I'm seeing.

"Can you help me off with this vest?" I hear the words, and I see Cane's lips move but it takes a minute for it to all come together in my head. I shake my head to regain my focus.

"Yep, you know Donna is going to have a herd of goats when she sees the blood all over her floor," is all I can think of to say as I undo the straps holding his vest on.

"Well hell hurry up. I don't want her handing me a sponge."

I nod and toss his vest on a nearby equipment cart. At the same moment, a member of the medical team appears and tells us Jack sent him.

"If you can stuff it and get the bleeding to slow down it'd be great. I can get down to the hospital in a bit to get it taken care of properly."

The medical assistant does as he's asked and after about five minutes, he tells Cane he's good to go.

Cane and I thanked him, and we took the stairs down to the detention level.

We walk past the desk and back to the large interrogation room at the end of the hallway to the open door. Jack and Kenzie are supervising the men as they strap down the prisoner.

Cane and I walk in, and Shaun looks up. "Boss you want his pants on or off?"

"On," is all I say.

He nods and they finish securing him on the table. It's much like an execution table, but both the arm and leg sections move independently.

Once the men have completed their tasks, I hear Jack say, "We need the room."

The men nod at me as they leave. Kenzie turns off all the lights except for the low light overhead and then shuts the door. There is a soft glow in the room. Depending on your circumstances I suppose they could be soothing or terrifying. The only people remaining in the room are Cane, Jack, and me.

Jack walks past and takes a position in a corner behind me. As Cane walks past his hand brushes mine. He leaves a heavy object behind and a pair of rubber gloves. He too takes up a position in a corner behind me. I pick up the remote from the cart nearby and push the button. It lifts the table to an upright position. I noticed someone was nice enough to loosen the draw string on the head bag. I step forward, take a deep breath, and put on the rubber gloves.

"Can you hear me?" my words echo off the walls.

"Do you know who I am?" is his ridiculous, screeching reply.

CYNICAL PLAY

"Well, I guess you can hear me. I want you to know, I *am* going to kill you. I want you to know, you are going to suffer. Not for minutes, not for an hour, but for days; even weeks. I am going to do everything in my power to keep you alive, so you continue to feel pain for as long as possible. I want you to know it is your father who has caused me to do this to you." I make sure to pronounce each word clearly and sharply.

"I don't know who you think you are, but my father will come for me. He's going to fucking kill you and all your little wanna-be commandos too!"

"Oh, I'm so hoping your father pops his head up looking for you. It'll make it much easier to separate it from his neck." I nod at Jack, and he turns on the spotlight directly over our guest. I reach up and yank the bag off his head.

The piece of shit is squinting and moving his head around quickly, I can only assume he's trying to get his bearings and attempting to figure out where he is. The bright light makes it almost impossible to see anything. "Who the fuck are you?" he yells into the room.

I step in front of him and look him right in the eyes. I use the knife Cane passed me, and I stab him two inches to the right of where his femoral artery should be. His mouth gapes open in pain and shock. I say to him in a voice full of rage and loathing, "I am Pandora you fuck tool." I removed the knife as quickly as I thrust it in. I shove my index and middle finger into the wound. He starts to scream and cry in agony.

I walked away to the door with my gloved hand covered in his blood. I scrawl Ryan's name on the door and turn all the lights in the room on. I handed the knife to Cane and told him to get the idiot patched up. As I open the door, I look back at the coward strapped to the table. I see him looking around the room and his reaction when he notices the large drain in the floor.

I say loud enough for our guest to hear me. "Mr. Kranston!" He lifts his head to look at me with tears and sweat running down his face.

"Welcome to the box!"

I decided to go to the medical floor for disinfectant for my hands in case anything snuck past the gloves. I would hate to catch cooties from the waste of oxygen. As I push through the double doors, one of the doctors stops me on my way to the sinks.

"Alex are you bleeding?" he asks with concern.

"Nope."

He nods and continues as if he never stopped me.

I wash up and decide I need to go up to my office. I need to check on the business. Even with all this personal drama going on, I can't let the business suffer.

I flop into my office chair and use the audio remote to turn on *Halestorm*. I put my hand on my head, leaned back, and listened to a few songs.

I hear the door to the stairs click open and Jacob appears with a tray. Once he sets down the tray on my desk, I see there is fancy seltzer water and homemade sweet potato chips. Jacob never misses a beat. He leaves two files on the edge of my desk and walks out as quietly as he walked in.

I open the first file and it's a missing person. It's a referral from a previous client. I know we need to look at this case now. If we are involved it means local law enforcement have done all they can, and the feds are

CYNICAL PLAY

doing what they can, but there is only so much manpower they can dedicate to something like this. Once too much time has passed, they must reallocate manpower to more recent cases. I read the entire file and make notes on the inside front cover, so I don't forget anything when I discuss it with Jack.

I picked up the desk phone and hit the autodial for Bowman. He's the best tracker I know. I'll have him start on this and if he finds anything, we can act on it or pass it back to the feds.

"Hey Alex, what'd you lose?"

"Bowman, a rich man's wife has gone missing. It has enough traction for us to get involved as the feds have run out of places to look. If you could give it a once over and let me know if you found anything, I would appreciate it."

"Sure, I can be there in thirty."

"See you then."

I hung up the phone as my office door opened. Jack looks in and sees me in my chair and shakes his head.

"Don't shake your head too hard old man. I don't want dust all over my floor."

He chuckles and sits down in his usual chair in front of my desk. I threw the missing woman's file at him.

"I have already spoken to Bowman; he'll be here shortly to get the file. If you would please read it, and make any additional notes, I'd appreciate it."

"Sure. Jacob mentioned he gave you two files."

"I've only managed to get to one so far."

I open the second file, and I almost throw up all over my desk.

"Christ Alex are you ok!" Jack exclaims, "You look like you saw a ghost."

I collect myself, close the file and push it over to Jack. "You better read this first."

He opens it and curses. "Why would Jacob give you this? The fuckin' fires on the island aren't even cold yet." He reaches for the intercom to call Jacob. I reach out and stop him from pushing the button.

"Jacob doesn't read the files. He has his own demons and doesn't need to wake any of them with our work. He only delivers them. There's no need to get mad at anyone. I'm not ready to see another client in a jersey. To be fair, I should have had you look at these first."

"Alex, you don't have to do any of this right now. I'll take care of it."

"Really, Jack. Now how the fuck would it look? I lose my shit and then I can't work. What am I supposed to do, take to my bed like some damn debutante?"

"What the hell does 'take to my bed' even mean? What weird movie did you watch on the plane?"

"Shut up." Is my only response.

Jack opens the folder and nods. "It's a protection detail for another rugby player. The guy has a stalker. Whoever it is has the means and funds to be able to stalk him even when he travels internationally. There's a bit of good news. He's currently on holiday, staying with his family, but will need protection once he returns. So, it looks like we might have a week or so before we're needed."

I reached for the phone and hit auto dial. "Boss?" is all I get over the speaker.

"Kenzie, please stop by the office when you have a moment."

"Yep," is his response before the connection ends.

Jack reaches over to grab a sweet potato chip, and I slap his hand. "Hey!" he yelps pulling his hand back.

"Hey nothing. You always bang on about the dirty hippy chips and now you try and take one. If you want some, call Jacob and ask him to make you some."

Jack sits back and crosses his arms over his chest. I think he might be pouting. The knock on the door doesn't surprise either of us.

"Come in," I yell.

Kenzie comes in and takes the other chair in front of my desk. Jack hands him the file. He flinches slightly when he opens it; collects himself and looks at me.

"What would you like me to do?"

"I need you to take this file and a three-man team. Meet with the contacts, in whatever location is convenient for them, and let us know what kind of detail this is going to require. Keep us in the loop."

"You got it."

Kenzie punches Jack in the arm and leaves. I push the chips towards Jack, and we continue to discuss the missing person file until Bowman arrives. There's another knock on the door but we both know it can't be the tracker already.

"Come in," we say at the same time.

Cane opens the door and makes his way towards my desk but doesn't sit down. "Things are underway downstairs. The white coat weirdos asked if the Crypt Keeper could give them a call when he has a minute."

"Funny, kid," Jack chuckles. "I'll see them. It's less creepy sometimes if I don't have to listen to them on the phone. The tall one is a bit of a mouth breather, it makes it weird if I don't pay for the phone call."

I shake my head as Jack snags a large hand full of chips and leaves the room. I motion for Cane to sit down but he continues to stand.

"Kenzie asked if I was interested in heading out with him. I told him I wanted to check if I was needed here first."

I take a deep breath and look at him. "I think joining Kenzie would be a good idea. Things here will be calm until we can contact the idiot's father."

He nods and leaves my office without another word.

I look around my desk and see a I have a phone message from Kelly, I can't recall if we have anything in the works at the title company, but I make a note to circle back and call her. I decided I can't be at my desk any longer, so I pushed through the side door and start up the stairs. I make it about halfway up when I realize I'm crying. I slide down the wall and sit down on the steps. I don't know how long I was sitting there but I must have fallen asleep. When I open my eyes, I find a blanket over my arms. Jacob really does need a raise.

I pick myself up, drag the blanket behind me and finish the climb to my flat. I open the door to a sparsely lit, chilly, quiet space. I manage a shower without further drama. I'm too tired to get dressed so I threw on underclothes and a robe. I emerge into the living room to find Jack standing beside the kitchen island eating something I'm sure Jacob left for me.

"Jacob called me when he found you on the stairs."

The room starts to spin a bit and before I hit the floor Jack catches me. I break down in a sobbing, screaming choking mess. Jack holds on to me as I crumple to the floor. He doesn't say anything, he holds on to me while I have a complete meltdown. When I start taking deep breaths again, I lay down and put my head on his legs. He sits with me and remains silent.

"You need to eat."

"I will."

"Jacob brought you some more of those hippy chips."

"Ok."

"You know this is a natural reaction to something like this, right?"

"I thought I was past the worst of it and then I saw the damn file. It's not as bad as the first bus which ran over me, but being side swiped by the second one was rough."

"I was trying to beat you to your office. To be fair I didn't know we had a case with another footballer, I wanted to make sure you were at least close to being over the worst of it before you came across anything even remotely similar."

"I appreciate it, but I think it's better for me to lose my shit privately."

"Yeah, I would hate to lose a room full of good men because they saw you showing you have feelings."

I pinch his leg, push myself upright and sit up against the couch next to him. Jack laughs and pushes his shoulder into mine. I stand up and hold my hand out to help him off the floor. We both make our way to the island in the kitchen. I sit on one of the stools and Jack gets us both something to drink.

"I didn't even make it to the name on the file for the protection detail."

"James Hannibal."

"Well, sounds ominously manly. Oh crap, did anyone meet with Bowman?"

"Yeah, I called him when I headed downstairs earlier. We talked about the missing woman, and he said he'd call with any updates."

Jack grins and shakes his head. He grabs his beer, the chips, and motions his head toward the couch. I pick up my water but nothing to eat. I'm still not ready for solid food yet. We sit on the couch like the two old friends we are, and watch *Bob's Burgers* because… Why not?

CHAPTER 4

I wake up on the couch with my tongue stuck to the roof of my mouth and my eyes feel like they're made of sandpaper. I can make out through my blurry dry contacts I'm alone on the couch. With each stretch I can feel and hear every bone crack. I carefully get up and make my way to the bathroom. My contacts are all but useless given, I slept in them, so I proceed carefully to the bathroom. I'm even more elated my flat is always clean, and Jacob never moves the furniture, so I navigate by muscle memory.

Safely in the bathroom I remove and throw my contacts in the trash. I make sure to start all the shower heads. As the bathroom starts to fog up, I finish brushing my teeth and throw yesterday's clothes onto the floor short of the hamper.

With my shower concluded I finish the lotion and taming my hair routine. Upon exiting the bathroom, I find three selections of clothing on the bed. I chose a black tank top, worn jeans, and steel toed boots. As I sit putting on my boots, I try not to think about anything. It's harder than it seems, thinking about nothing. I lean over, rest my elbows on my knees and collect myself. On a deep breath I stand up.

I found Jacob in the kitchen cooking. Jack, Kenzie, and Cane are sitting together at the large table eating quietly. I can see there is no bacon on the table. Jacob will not put it out until I get to the table, but they're eating everything else. I take my seat at the head of the table and Jacob sets down the hot plate of bacon near my end of the table. I push it towards Jack. He takes a handful and passes the plate down to Kenzie. He takes a healthy number of pieces and passes the plate to Cane. No one is talking which is fine by me.

The quiet's broken by Jacob as he starts the blender going on the counter. Jacob returns to the table and sets down a travel glass with a brown chocolate concoction in it. I'm sure it's full of vitamins and protein and good for someone. I nod and he walks back to the kitchen to make more food for the others. When I'm confident about my voice I start to ask questions.

"Kenzie, how did the meeting go in regard to Mr. Hannibal?"

He finishes chewing and takes a drink of his energy drink. "It went well. There's a legitimate threat, and we'll need to provide a seven-man team."

"Ok, it sounds like you have it under control" I say making sure to concentrate on every word.

"Boss, there's one thing his people requested," Kenzie adds.

"What?" I look at Jack because I can't imagine what they could want Kenzie couldn't provide at the meeting.

Jack shrugs in response. "Mr. Hannibal's people said they want the best we have."

"What the fresh fuck do they mean? I sent you. You are the best we have. Fuck them. Let them get their client shot or skinned or whatever this stalker wants to do to him."

When Jack stops laughing, he chimes in, "Maybe we should meet with them and find out what the disconnect is, before we throw their client to the wolves."

"No!" is my curt response.

I see Cane reach his hand out across the table. Jack reaches out and passes him a fifty-dollar bill. I shake my head at them both and snatch the bill right out of Cane's outstretched hand. Kenzie is laughing so hard he's choking a little and his neon green energy drink is coming out his nose.

"Alex, we should agree to a meeting and require they bring Mr. Hannibal. He isn't aware of what the ass hats working for him are asking for." Jack says to bring us back on topic.

"Vote, who thinks we should take the meeting?" I ask, knowing what the answer will be. They all raised their hands. "You know voting to take the meeting, to see if I will shoot or stab one of them, isn't the point."

"Ha, she said point!" Kenzie laughs at his own statement.

I pick up my phone and the meal replacement shake, mostly to make Jacob happy. "I'm going down to have a chat with the bait. Kenzie set up the meeting and we'll circle back to this."

"You got it boss," his reply comes over a mouth full of eggs.

I choose to use the front door and wave at the guys at the desks. As I reach out to push the down button on the elevator, I see there's already a hand pushing the button. I look back and find Cane standing off my left shoulder.

The doors open, we step on and ride down to the detention level without a word. We exited the elevator in the same silence.

Barney is on the desk and stands as soon as he sees us. "Mornin' Boss," he says in his usual cheery downhome drawl.

"How are things down here Barney?" I ask, with as much pleasantry as I can muster.

"I've fed and watered the animals. The new occupant, at the end, has been whimpering and cussin' all night. Every time someone went in to visit with him there were promises of cash and threats of death."

"Well, it's good to hear he's still full of piss and vinegar. Should be enough remaining to leak out of the holes I'm about to put in him. Did Jack's weirdos leave any of their tools in the room?"

"I think so. They went in with one of their covered carts, but they left without it."

"Good deal, thanks Barney." I say patting him on the back.

"Boss?" He asks.

"Yep?" I say turning to give him my attention.

"Don't get any of him on you" he says with his usual grin.

"Thanks for the reminder." I wave at him as we start down the hallway.

We make our way past all the solitary cells. At the end of the hallway is the door to the box. Next to the door is a large standing metal cabinet. I open the door and pull out a hoodie and a clear mask to go over my face. I take the little blue jar of mentholated rub and put a little under my nose. Cane declines a hoodie and a mask, but he accepts the jar. I shrug, enter my code into the security panel next to the door, press my index finger to the print scanner, and lean forward to look in the retina scanner. I hear the door unlock, and Cane is kind enough to pull open the heavy soundproof door for me.

We walk in and the smell isn't as bad as I thought it would be. The industrial fans and drain are doing their job. The floor is wet so clearly Jack's people used the power washer when they finished. It's appreciated. I put on my hoodie and mask. Cane uncovers the cart left by Jack's mad scientists. He pushes it closer to the table and hands me the remote. I quickly locate the button to tilt the table upright. I don't want to have to lean over this idiot to see him.

The poor stupid bastard was either asleep or unconscious. He looks around the room and realizes it wasn't a nightmare as he's still our guest. He seems to focus on us, and a look of confusion comes over his face. I raise the mask up and rest it on my head. I can see his brain is trying to figure out where he has seen me before.

"Remember me Mr. Kranston?" I ask calmly.

He attempts to laugh, I think. It's a bit of a gurgling sound. "What's with the mask? I already saw your face and I'll tell my father about all of this."

I waved to Cane. He picks up the hood from the table and walks around behind our guest. In one quick motion he places the hood over Mr. Kranston head and ties it at the back of his neck.

"I'm not trying to disguise myself. I'm going to wear the mask, so I don't get any bits of you on me. Let's start the entertainment, shall we? Not to worry, the last part was rhetorical." I hear Cane laugh at my last comment.

I pull the mask down over my face and choose a hand drill with a long bit from the cart. I pull the trigger to make sure it's working. I glance at Mr. Kranston knowing he's confused as he can't see what I have in my hand or what body part I'm heading toward. I walk to the table and he's trying his best to get as far from me as he can. As he's strapped to the table the attempt is futile.

I grab his left knee and feel around for the small space where the patella slides over the knee joint. I place the bit right at the gap and press the go button. The expensive suit pants shred and I'm sure bits of fabric end up inside the wound. His screams echo off the walls as I push the bit deep into his knee. Instead of reversing the drill I simply yank the bit straight out. It took me three attempts to get it completely out. I must have hit a bone somewhere, but I finally got the bit out, which is the important part as I intend to use it again.

Since I can't see his face because of the hood, the sound of his agony brings me peace if only for a second or two. I feel for the same space on the other side of his knee. I place the bit on the skin and hit the go button again. His screaming is the soundtrack as blood and additional tissue comes out as I remove the bit. Again, I'm at peace with my actions. I put the drill, with the blood, bone fragments and tissue, back on the cart.

There are so many tools on the cart, it's hard to make a choice of what to use next. Then I see what looks like some kind of surgical spreader and a pair of simple kitchen shears. I walk back to him, only to see his sweat, snot and tears mixing as they run down his face and out from under the hood. I look down at the holes in his knee and I know the items I chose will work nicely. I realize I need a direct light and damn if Cane hasn't moved to stand behind me with a mag light.

I put the spreader in the wound on the inside of the moron's knee and turn the handle, so the skin comes apart. I can see white stringy bits among other internal parts. The screaming is almost constant at this point. I'm honestly surprised he hasn't passed out. I wait for the screams to die down a bit before I stick the shears inside the wound and take a big snip out of the stringy white bits. The screams increase and become more piercing, Cane sucks in a little whistle.

With my gloved hand I poke my fingers in the bleeding wound to see if I can find some more things to trim. I find three larger bits, with a rubber band texture. I figure, since I'm here, why not give these a snip as well. I poke the shears in the hole and cut without pause. With a final high pitch scream the room is completely quiet.

I look up and the poor fucker has finally passed out, but not before vomiting a bit down the front of himself. Cane places the light back on the cart and reaches up to remove the hood from the unconscious man. Pieces of vomit, caught in the hood, fall out onto the floor.

Cane grunts and looks down. "He's out cold and still managed to get vomit on my boots. When he wakes up, I'm going to punch him in his other fucking knee."

I laugh so hard I lose my balance a bit. I collect myself and put the various tools back on the cart.

CYNICAL PLAY

I point towards the cabinet near the door. "The power washer is in there. If you would please clean off the floor and don't forget your boots. I'm going to ring the doc and tell him his patient is bleeding again."

Cane nods and makes his way to the cabinet to get out the power washer.

I push the red button on the intercom, it's the direct line to the doctor's office. "Doc, you there?"

"Yes, Alex. Did you need something?" His reply is calm.

"Yep, the guy in the box is bleeding and dribbling vomit on the floor. I think he may need stitches." I hear the doc take a deep breath.

"Alex, you know I hate vomit." His tone is both resigned and exasperated.

"I know doc, it's rough but not to worry Cane will clean up the sick puddle for you." I pressed the button to end the chat with the doctor and turned to find Cane putting the power washer away. He clearly washed off his boots, but Mr. Kranston got a good deal of water as well. I removed the mask as well as the hoodie and put them both in the incinerator chute. Cane opens the door, and I see the doctor heading our way.

As I walk past him the doctor asks "Alex, is the area needing stitches obvious?"

I nod, "Oh yea."

Cane holds the door for the doctor and his assistants. I can hear the doctor asking one of his assistants if the subject is dead. Cane holds the door until we hear confirmation, he's still alive and then he lets the heavy door shut.

I wave at Barney as we pass the desk and get on the elevator. Cane and I both leaned back against the wall, arms crossed across our chests.

He looks down as the elevator starts to move. "Boss?"

"Yeah?" I close my eyes and lean my head back against the wall.

"You got Kranston on your boots."

CHAPTER 5

Cane's phone rings as the elevator slows. "Yeah, brother she's with me. What's going on? We're on our way."

I look over at him waiting for him to tell me what's going on. "You're needed in the tech cave. It sounds like father-of-the-year has reached out."

I pull off my boots and leave them on the elevator. We make our way quickly down the long hallway to the secure IT offices. I put my eye to the scanner, and we waited for the sound of the door unlocking before Cane reached forward to open it. Kyle is at the security desk and enters the code to let us into the back-office space. I can see Jack, Kenzie and Benji waiting in the large briefing room in the center of the office. Kenzie seems a bit on edge, but Jack is leaning back in a chair with his feet up and arms behind his head. Not one of them says a word about my lack of shoes.

I confront my IT guy. "Ok Benji, what's going on?"

"Boss, we have a video message forwarded to us by a what I can only say is perhaps a distant business associate."

"I want the name of this distant business associate as soon as possible. We need to see why they'd function as a go-between for this reprobate." I look at Jack and know he's thinking the same thing. "Benji and Kenzie, see what you can find out."

CYNICAL PLAY

"Let's see it." I motion with my hand for Benji to play it.

Benji points to the giant screen over my shoulder and I turn to see the screen turn from black to blue.

A man appears on the screen. He's very well dressed, which is not a surprise. He has a tumbler filled with amber liquid in his hand, and I can hear the ice chiming in the glass. He's calmly sitting back in a large black tufted leather chair and seems very sure of himself. He looks into the camera and starts to speak. "I decided to send this message to you through someone I felt sure you would have come across given the type of work you do. My people found very telling details about you and your operation when we were perusing your island.

"So let me start with an introduction. My name is John D. Kranston, JD to my friends. I was unable to locate my son and his only surviving security escort told me of the crass way he was taken from his hotel suite." He shakes his head as he takes a sip of the liquor in his glass.

"It only made sense to assume you have taken him. I'm not sure why you felt it was necessary to continue this tit for tat. I was simply repaying the kindness you showed my family when you took my younger brothers' life." He takes a drink and appears to acknowledge someone else in the room he's filming from. He clears his throat and begins to speak to the camera again.

"You have 48 hours to return my son. I even understand if he's not completely well. I'm sure you have been employing less than civilized methods to find out where I am. We will let this slide, for now. However, let me make one thing perfectly clear. If after 48 hours I do not have my son back, I will come for you, and you will wish you were on your island with whoever the poor soul was you had staying there." This last part is said with a wave of his hand and then the screen goes blue and then black again.

I turn slowly to find only Jack and Cane looking at me. Kenzie appears to have left the room and Benji appears to be trying to make himself look as small as possible at the desk.

"Benji?" I say as calmly as possible, after all I'm not mad at him.

"Yes boss," comes a less than confident voice from behind the array of monitors.

"In the pause where he looks at someone or something in the room. Find out who or what it was. I want to know all the background sounds and I want to see all the reflections off the hard surfaces."

"Yes boss." Benji starts furiously working his keyboard and mouse.

"I'll be at the range." I turn and leave the room, using the stairs to get to the range. I stop six times to collect myself before I push through the door and find Kevin inside the cage.

"Hey Alex, wha'cha in the mood for today?"

"Sniper rifle."

"OK…" He takes a moment to consider the many options we have. "Are you looking for long distance or really long distance?"

I consider his question. "How about one ready for anything."

CYNICAL PLAY

He winks and disappears into his stacks of weapons. About five minutes later he reappears with a long case and large box of ammunition.

"Here you go Alex. Use the stall on the end. It's the only one set up to take these kinds of rounds. Oh, and you have company, Kenzie is in his usual stall."

I nod and grab a pair of safety goggles off the shelf. I search my front pockets and can't find my ear plugs. I look at Kevin and he has his hand out with a new pair. I thanked him and picked up the heavy case from the counter along with the ammunition. Kevin buzzes me through the door.

Walking past the stalls I noticed two occupied; everyone must maintain their weapons proficiency. I also see Kenzie standing in his usual spot. I walked past him without a word of acknowledgment, and I set the gun case and ammo box on the safe table. I unpack the weapon and assemble what I need. I take a handful of rounds with me to the firing position. It took the better part of two hours to familiarize myself with the weapon. When I got up and turned to put the weapon back in the case, I found Jack leaning against the safe table with his arms crossed.

I calmly and quietly packed the weapon away, picked up the case and mostly empty ammo box, and walked past Jack without a word. I noticed Kenzie was no longer in his preferred stall. I knew Jack was behind me, but I didn't slow down. I exited the range and put my new earplugs in my pocket.

"Please clean this," I placed the case on the counter, "and put it to the side for me. I imagine I'm going to need it soon."

Kevin winks, "You got it."

I take the stairs back up to my office without turning around or acknowledging Jack in my wake. As I reach the door to go to my office, I realize I never put shoes on. I take a detour up a floor to get some. As I walk past the security desks and into my flat, I notice Jack has given up. Jacob is inside cleaning, but I'm on a mission to get shoes. I grab new socks and a pair of Sketchers out of the closet.

When I get to my desk the light on my phone is blinking. I hit the message button and Benji's voice fills the room. "Boss, I sent you the sounds and images you asked for from my first few scrubs of the video. I'm still putting it through other programs and Kacey is working on a new algorithm to pick up even more details, if possible. I will forward any current information as soon as we find it. Also, I located the potential source JD Kranston used to send the video to us. He was indirectly involved with the theatre case we participated in last year. A politician who would have been in the debriefing, by the police on a 'need to know' basis."

I pulled out the top drawer and placed my thumb in the print scanner. The computer screen comes to life, and I click on the email icon to look at the information Benji sent.

I use the remote on my desk to turn on the giant screens in my office. I open the attachments and push them to the big screens so I can get a better look. Each photo is marked up so I can clearly see what they found. Also, there could be location information based on whatever sounds and images they detected. One of the last attachments is a map with all the markers on it. It's

CYNICAL PLAY

giving me mostly Tennessee or Georgia. I will leave all this for Jack. He can play man of the map. I want to know who or what distracted the bad man in the chair.

I open the email about the source dear old dad used to deliver his message. As I look at the name, it only confirms politicians don't have a clue when to keep their mouths shut. He thought if he didn't give out our contact information, but instead forwarded JD's email to us, there'd be no issue. I'm sure it was motivated by the hope of a substantial contribution to his reelection fund. Unfortunately, I can't shoot him, at least not outright, but I can remove him from the gene pool, and I will, but later when this is over.

I went back and read the report. There's a voice in the background, and it says something to the effect of 'still nothing sir'. Well, I suppose it's good news for us.

When Jack finally makes an appearance, I'm sitting at the large conference table still studying the photos. He takes a seat across from me and leans forward on the table.

"So, what kind of crazy do you have banging around in your head?"

Before I can answer there's a knock on the door. Jack yells for whoever it is to enter. Cane opens the door and Jack waves him in. He shuts the door and takes a seat next to Jack.

Jack points at me. "Alex was about to share her master plan with me."

I look at both and calmly say, "We are going to give the man back his son."

Cane is clearly confused, and Jack has a look of suspicion on his face. I make more notes about the photos and look up to find the two of them still staring at me. "What?"

Jack squints and taps his index finger on the table. "What do you mean *what*? What the fuck are you up to? We went to all this trouble to track this kid down and abduct him. You have already started to poke him with sharp objects. Now, you're going to give him the fuck back. He hasn't even told us anything, has he?"

I look at Cane and make a hand motion for him to say whatever he's thinking. He puts his hands up in supplication. "Hey, I'm here to follow instructions. You say we give him back then we give him back."

Jack punches him in the arm. "Chicken."

I take a deep breath and look at Jack and Cane. "You have 24 hours to get any information you can from the moron, starting now."

"Jack, I assume we can arrive at the drop off point within the 48-hour timeline, even with the 24 hours I've given you to interrogate him further?" I question. Jack nods but still looks unconvinced there isn't more here than he's being told.

"Cane, before we leave, you will oversee preparing the spawn for transport. I want him tied up like he's Hannibal Lector. I want a bag over his head and earplugs covered by sound canceling headphones. I don't want him to be able to tell dear old dad anything about this place."

Cane nods, gets up from the table and heads back to the box. Jack is still squinting at me.

"You can stop with the Clint Eastwood stare. We're giving the kid back and we're going to come at this from another angle." I leaned back in my chair.

CYNICAL PLAY

"What's with the sniper rifle?" Jack asks, not convinced by my explanation.

"I didn't know I needed to explain myself."

"Look it's going to be hard to have your back if I don't know what your brain has planned." His irritation was obvious.

"Well how about you get on these maps and figure out where daddy dearest is. Or take your butt down to the box and see if you can get any additional information from the son. Then you can worry about having my back because then we'll have a reason to go outside." I go back to looking through the files Benji sent me. I hear Jack call Cane and tell him to get all the details he can from the kid and that he's going to stay and help me search for the father's location.

"Oh, one other thing," I add. "The source who potentially functioned as the go-between for daddy Kranston, was one of our local politicians. The police briefed him on the theatre debacle we worked on last year, in the need-to-know group. Good news, *we* never personally briefed him. As usual he doesn't have a clue about the damage he could cause if our internal security weren't as tight as it is. We will be showing him an exit from this current version of his life. However, it will have to wait until we have taken care of the current situation." Jack doesn't say anything but rolls his eyes in frustration. I go back to reading the reports.

Jack pulls the maps and notes towards himself. He looks at me one more time and shakes his head before he gets to work.

I take a seat at my desk as there are other parts of the business needing my attention. I have an email from Bowman. "Jack, listen to this. Bowman says he located the missing woman."

Jack waves his hand signaling me to continue but not taking his eyes off the maps.

"Bowman says he took the dogs with him to the vacant land the husband owns through his business. He says it took the dogs about an hour to signal a hit. He called his contact with the Feds and so far, they have found two more bodies on the property. He says he's going to send his invoice to the Feds since this is going to be their circus."

Jack looks up smirking. "I'm sure the Feds are thrilled."

I replied to Bowman's message and let him know we'll be sending a congratulations basket to him and the dogs as a thank you. I forward the message to Jacob so he can take care of it. I'm still laughing as Jack looks at me again and shakes his head as he goes back to study the maps.

After two and a half hours of updates and listening to more than ten of Jack's phone calls we get word from Benji. The location Jack has proposed in Montana, the day after tomorrow, has been confirmed by the receiving party. It's a random piece of land, owned by the government, miles away from anything. The plan is to return the moron son, track him back and then choose the best plan of attack.

There's a tap on the office door. "Enter," I respond.

CYNICAL PLAY

Cane enters and informs us his time in the box with Kranston's son has given us every location daddy Kranston usually stays and how he determines his schedule. "Unfortunately, the father is paranoid as hell and revamps his schedule every other month. His current schedule has been in place for a week. For now, he's in Palm Springs. I have his address."

"Definitely good news. We'll act on this as soon as we get done with the current mess we're in."

"One more thing, boss. The kid gave up his father's second in command. He was kind enough to tell us whatever his father knows this guy knows. Also, daddy dearest doesn't even pee without consulting this guy. It didn't sound like the son and the second get along, so we will need to run this guy to ground."

Jack agrees with Cane's assessment, and we all leave the office for our respective flats to sleep and get ready for tomorrow.

It's early, as I enter my office. I don't even get to sit down as Cane calls, and I answer on speaker. Jack enters the office as the phone rings and sits down in front of all his maps. Cane lets us know the prisoner is ready for transport as Jack looks up from the maps and nods.

I tell Cane to let the others know we are ready when they are, and Jack will be forwarding the needed information. We have decided to take a ten-man team. Everyone is in black, everyone will be wearing balaclavas, vests and everyone is going in heavily armed. The vehicles will be armor plated but only one will go to the exchange point.

Jack and I leave everything as is, in my office, and we assemble with the others in the garage. Cane emerges from the freight elevator with the spawn strapped to a gurney with a wheelchair laying on top of his body. He loads the hostage gurney and all into a waiting van. The rest of us load into the SUV's and make our way to the private airport.

Upon arrival I see Jack has called for our largest plane. It comes with six cages and floor chain restraints on more than 15 seats. Cane removes the straps from our guest and gets him into the wheelchair. He pushes the spawn onto the plane, gets him transferred and chained to his seat. I stop Jack by asking him who's going to take the guy to the drop. This gives the other guys time to load the equipment on the plane without Jack stopping every item to inspect it.

Once everything is on board, we join the others on the plane and it's only two hours to the isolated landing strip. As we exit the plane, there are three armored SUV's waiting for us. Each vehicle carries a driver and one additional man. I wave at the guys and Davis gets out of the last SUV and heads towards me with a smirk on his face. His other men help to unload the toys we brought with us.

"What's with the smirk," I ask interested.

He chuckles, "It appears the party we are meeting may have had other plans. We got here as soon as you called and watched as what I can only assume was a hired team of hitters take up spots last night."

I can't say I'm shocked, but I'm pissed, I didn't even think it was a possibility. I'm glad Davis was doing his job and mine. "So, what happened to this advance team?"

CYNICAL PLAY

Davis smiles, "Well considering we were here first, we made sure to set up our signal jammers. Jerome noticed through his scope when their communication equipment wouldn't work, they added heart monitors to their gear. So, he came up with a hell of an idea." I motion for him to continue.

"There were four of them. Since there is only really one point of access to get to the drop point, they decided to climb to the top of the ridge. We sent two of our snipers up behind each of them. It took some time, but they snuck up on them without issue." I don't interrupt him; I only raise my eyebrow.

Davis puts his hand up and continues. "The first man subdued the target while the second man placed one of these under the heart monitors on each shooter." I look down and see a plush dog toy. I look back to Davis.

"Jerome takes in strays and helps the local shelters. These things mimic a heartbeat and give off heat simulating another dog. He uses them with all his new intakes. He had a bunch in his truck. We strapped them to the bodies before we snuffed them, and the heart monitors didn't miss a beat."

Jack burst out laughing. "Fucking brilliant. Let Jerome know he'll be receiving a contribution to his animal saving enterprises." Jack walks off to get prepared, still laughing. He also took the dog toy with him.

I turn and look back at Davis. "Thank you for covering my ass on this one, I should've known this guy would send an advance team."

Davis looks at me and without missing a beat, "It's what we do. If those bastards had a team, instead of hiring some Rambo's, those guys on the ridge might have lived a bit longer."

I nod and he points over my shoulder. I turn and watch as Cane wheels our guest off the plane. Kenzie helps to load him in the lead truck. Once they secure him, they head over to where Jack and I are standing chatting about what comes next, once we find parent of the year's base of operation.

I make sure I have everyone's attention. "Okay, Jack is going to take the useless sack of bones to the drop. One of Davis's men will drive him out and Jack will open the door and put him at the drop. They'll then drive away and begin the task of tracking this fucker."

Kenzie raises his hand. I reach over and mess up his hair. He smiles, his joker's grin, and asks his question. "Why don't we put a tracker on the son?"

Jack answers him. "They're sure to find anything we try to put on or in the kid. Using marking technology will get us more targets. It will be activated once they make any type of biological contact with each other. It works like a virus."

Davis waves his hand, and I motion for him to go ahead. "We've also set up body heat cameras so we can have an accurate body count inside the cars or car they bring to the pickup."

I punch Davis, "Now you're trying to get a bonus." Davis laughs and hands Kenzie a small tablet showing all the body heat cameras. He also lets him know Benji already has the feed for these.

Kenzie grins, shrugs, and heads back to the truck to check his weapons one more time.

CYNICAL PLAY

"Cane, you will be lead in the second truck. I need you to make sure the video is clear and constant back to Benji. Since we are in the middle of nowhere, we need to make sure there are no interruptions to the feed. We need Benji to get us real time information on whoever this guy brings as back up. Should daddy's leash holder come with him, we need to get the best image of him as possible." He nods and makes a line for his vehicle.

Jack looks at me but doesn't say anything. "What, old man?" I ask with annoyance in my voice.

"If Cane is hunting the mystery man as well as any others and I'm taking this guy back to his daddy. What are you doing?" Jack says, trying not to sound suspicious.

"Easy, I'll be back here with Kenzie in case anyone needs anything."

Jack had something else to say but thought better of it. He pulls on his balaclava and heads to his truck.

Once he and Cane depart from the staging area, I put my hand out to Kenzie. "Give me your com."

Kenzie hands it to me without question. As I turned to walk back to one of the SUVs I tell Kenzie. "You can stay here with the plane or come with me. Your choice."

"With you." Is all he says before falling into step next to me.

I nod to Davis. He motions to two of his guys. They joined Kenzie and me. We all got into the third SUV and take off to a secondary location I found on the maps. I almost feel a little bad for Kenzie. He knew something was up and he had no way to stop it. I handed him back his com. I know I don't have to tell him to leave Cane and Jack out of this.

Davis gets us close enough to the drop where there will not be an issue with visibility. We want to be able to see the exchange, but we don't want anyone to see us. We park the SUV under a large rock overhang. Davis backs around a bend carefully so the rear of the SUV points out towards the exchange. We all get out and set up our positions. Kenzie prepares his weapon and doesn't ask any questions.

Monty, Davis's second in command, gets the rear of the SUV set up. He folds down the portable sound-proofing as well as a veil for the open back end. When he uncovers the sniper rifle, I hear Kenzie behind me, "Crap."

As I get ready to climb into the back of the SUV, I look up to see the heel of a boot sticking out the veil. Davis's other man was on top of the SUV with a sniper rifle pointed in the other direction. Once in the back of the SUV, I get into position and wait to hear from Davis. He and Monty are in a position to make sure no one sneaks up on us. Kenzie rubs his hands over his face and gets in the SUV with me to assume the position as my spotter.

We spent the next 30 minutes waiting to see Jack come into our line of sight to make the drop. We went up the mountain and Jack had to go down through the valley. I knew his trip would take longer. I can read maps too.

I watch through a small monitor linked to a camera on the top of the SUV Monty has set up. Taking a moment to look through my scope I see Jack lift the prisoner out of the SUV and sit him on a rock in the middle of the empty space. He removes all the restraints and the hood. He leaves him with a couple large bottles of water, and Jack being Jack, gives him the middle finger before getting back in the SUV. Jack pulls away quickly and is soon a dust cloud going back through the valley.

We wait another hour before a silver Mercedes appears at the drop spot. Three of the doors open and an equal number of imposing men exit the car weapons out. The one who exited the front passenger door, steps to the rear of the car. He opens the door and outsteps dear old dad. My eyes tell me there is another person in the car, but my brain is focusing too hard on the task at hand to process the information. I ask Kenzie, "How many bodies are inside the car?"

Without missing a beat he answers, "Two confirmed, boss; there are two people still inside the car."

At least I know I'm not losing my mind. "Kenzie confirm the identity of dear old dad if you would please." I'm trying to remain calm, but my brain is moving too fast to focus on more than one thing.

Kenzie takes a deep breath after completing the facial recognition scan, "The light is green boss. I say again the light is green."

I look through the scope and find my target. I concentrate on my breath and think about the heartbeats. I take a few deep breaths, and on the seventh exhalation, I squeeze the trigger. I keep my eye on the scope and watch the shock on dear old dad's face as he realizes he's covered in bits of his son's head.

I take one more look at the scene and see a head appear over the rear door of the Mercedes. We don't waste any time. We move in a hurricane of motion. The guy on the roof of the SUV slides down the front taking his and our cover with him. Kenzie is out of the back and brings in the camera and any ground cover. I'm breaking down the weapon as Davis and Monty get in the front seats and start the SUV. Kenzie closes the back and he and the roof guy jump into the rear seats, and we head back to the plane.

We were all in radio silence and we remained so until we got back to the plane. Jack comes flying out of his SUV at me and I can see out of the corner of my eye Cane has hit the ground running. I put my hand up to stop Cane. He halts where he is and waits for further instructions. I can tell he's not happy as the situation unfolds. Jack grabs me by the vest, and I can see he is furious.

"What the fuck were you thinking? You could have gotten us all killed. You should have shot the old man while you were at it. Damn it, Alex!"

I'm not tense. I'm letting Jack get it all out. Despite the spittle landing on my face, I can see around us the guys are loading the plane, and the locals are exiting the scene as fast as they can. Kenzie is standing in front of Cane. I'm assuming he's trying to explain to him this is none of their business.

"Well Alex?" Jack asks, as he starts to run out of steam.

I look him right in the eye and in my coldest tone I tell him the truth. "I told him I would return his son. I kept my word. I never promised him he'd be alive."

CHAPTER 6

"Fucking semantics, Alex, seriously!" He's still yelling and shaking me. "He's going to fucking come after us with everything he has! He's going to hunt us like animals!" He's still yelling but he's out of steam.

I can see out of the corner of my eye Kenzie has managed to get Cane onto the plane and remains at the doorway to make sure he doesn't try to exit. I'm sure I can hear Cane throwing his gear around inside the plane.

I look back to focus on Jack. He releases my vest, and I lean forward to whisper in his ear.

"The mother fucker gave the order which left Ryan to die alone on the island. Not to mention the number of our men killed trying to keep him safe. Think about it Jack! I mean really think about it. I had his brother killed to enforce our internal policy, which Jim Lee knew would happen if we found out. He made his choice when he started having sex with the doctor. This asshole had Ryan killed, as well as twenty-eight of our men. This was not one of yours for one of mine types of exchanges. This was a tool bag trying to show us how big his balls are. I never had any intention of letting any of them live. The fact he got to see his son one more time was a fucking gift, and it will be the last."

Jack pulls back from me, and I can see the concern and understanding in his eyes. I don't know if the concern were for me only, or for the potential body count this could result in. Either way I made my point.

I clap him on the shoulder, "Let's go. We have things to do." He does the only thing he can. He nods and after a deep breath falls in step next to me.

We get on the plane, and I walk past a seething Cane. Kenzie already has his headphones on playing a casino game on his tablet. I go into the bathroom to clean up. As I close the door, I can hear Jack tell the pilot we're ready and then I hear the ice clank into the tumbler.

When I come out of the bathroom Cane is waiting for me. "Yes?" I say still drying my hands.

"You could have told me what was going on." He says with as much calm as he's capable of under the circumstances.

"I suppose, but you work for me. Given this, I am not in any way obligated to tell you anything. In the larger scheme of things, you had your assignment, and I had a task I needed to complete."

Cane looks like he's going to explode but he manages to change gears. "You know putting Kenzie in that situation wasn't fair."

"I would agree with your statement. However, as I said, I had a task to complete and he's the best on the eye. He had a choice to stay on the plane. He made the choice to come with me."

Cane scratches his short blonde beard, grabs my shoulders, and shakes me. Not anything like Jack had, but enough for me to understand his meaning.

"Alex if they had men up on the ridge they could have exploded your head like a melon."

"It's interesting you think I would not take precautions to prevent such a situation."

He nods and I walk away from him not really concerned about how he feels. I grab a bag of gummy worms from the pantry shelf and drop them on Kenzie's chest on my way to my seat. He smiles and gives me a thumbs up and goes back to playing his game. I find my seat, recline, and try to turn off my brain.

When we land Jack says he'll be back later. He takes the keys from one of the drivers who has come to pick us up. He speeds out of the private airport without looking back.

"Is grandpa going to go see the naked women?" Kenzie asks as he tries to ease the tension.

I laugh and look around. "Since we are now short a truck let's get this stuff packed as best we can. Kenzie you may have to ride on top of the cases."

"Grandpa's an asshole." Kenzie says picking up a couple of ammo cases.

We all laugh and finish loading the equipment.

When we get back to the garage, I drop everything on the ground outside the cage except my clothes. The elevator seems to take forever to get me to my flat. When the doors slide open, I push away from the wall and wave at the guard on the desk. He pushes the button to open the door for me. Even then the damn thing is still heavy. I make it as far as the couch. I lay down and I'm out.

I stir awake to the sound of my phone ringing and keep my eyes closed and paw around the couch trying to find the damn thing. I finally got frustrated enough to open my eyes, looked around and found the stupid thing on the floor. I reach down and slide my finger on the screen to answer it.

"What?"

"Boss, it's Benji."

Again, I ask, "What?"

"We received another message." Benji replies.

"Have you called Jack?" I sit up, completely awake now.

"Yes, but all I get is voicemail. I called Cane and he's on his way. He doesn't know where Jack is either."

"Shit, send Kenzie to me and tell Cane I'll meet him in your office in 20 minutes." I try to prioritize my thoughts while my brain catches up with me.

"Yes, Boss." Benji hangs up.

I stand and start removing clothes as I hit the bedroom and then the shower. I leave the bathroom doors slightly open and turn on all the shower heads. I work through getting clean as fast as I can, and I hear a voice in the outer rooms somewhere. "Kenzie are you out there?"

Kenzie must still be in the living room because he's yelling. "Yes boss. Benji said you wanted to see me."

I can barely hear him. "Kenzie, come in the bedroom so I can speak to you without yelling,"

I heard him knock on the bathroom door.

"I need you to find the old man." I say over the water spray, trying not to drown myself.

"He doesn't move fast. How the hell can he be lost?" Kenzie chuckles in response.

"I need him here. Go track his ass down."

"Yes, Boss," is all he says before knocking on the door again and leaving the room.

I dress and leave my hair to dry naturally as I run down the stairs two at a time. I push my way into Benji's private office. Cane is already sitting on one of the extra stools.

"You hear from Jack?" I asked Cane.

"Nope; why, Benji asked me about him too." Cane stands. "What's going on?"

"Benji can't reach him, and I've sent Kenzie out to check the regular places. It's possible he got drunk and passed out somewhere." I check my phone for word from Kenzie.

"You know it's a real possibility he's not ready to talk to you. After what happened he's still pissed." Cane sits back down on the stool.

I take a deep breath and shake my head in disgust. "If pouting is his reason, then he can stay wherever he is. We don't have time for any childish, tantrum bullshit. He can be as mad as he wants when this is all over. Hell, I would be willing to spar with him without any protective gear if it will help him feel better. But if he's pulling this crap while we are knee deep in this shit, I'll shoot him myself."

Cane rubs the top of his head and nods. "Benji let's see what you got before she shoots me for saying dumb things."

Poor Benji is doing his best to hide behind his monitors. "On the screen," is all he says pointing behind us.

CYNICAL PLAY

The same man who appeared buttoned up and put together is now ghostly in appearance. I notice he still has bits of his son on him. If I'm honest, it makes me feel better.

He takes a long drink of the clear liquid swishing around in the highball glass in his shaking hand before speaking. "You have no honor. You are less than a coward. You are dead…all of you are dead. I'm going to hunt you down and remove your insides while you are still alive. I'm going to flay your skin and show it to you from across the room." He pronounces each syllable in each word with venom. He drains the glass with some of the liquid dribbling out of his mouth and throws the glass. We can hear it crash against a wall. He rubs his face with both hands and looks back into the camera.

"I have already taken one of your precious pieces. I will be sure to send you the video of his screams as we remove his eyes and teeth, one at a fucking time." He gets up and knocks over the camera. Right before he steps on it, we can hear screaming off camera.

I turn to look at Cane and for a moment we both have the same thought. Cane takes off without further comment.

"Benji, find Jack. Track his phones, the truck he took, his credit cards and I mean all of them. Call Kenzie and Cane as soon as you find anything. Also, get me the images and sounds off this video as soon as you can. Send everything even if it's a duplicate of the previous messages."

"Yes Boss, right away." He starts to type, and programs open with alarming speed on his multiple monitors.

I take the stairs two at a time up to the boardroom. I push one of Jack's pre-sets on the phone in the middle of the table. The phone only rings once when a noticeably quiet, two pack a day, voice answers the call.

"Asshole, I'm working," is the greeting I get.

"Conroy. Jack's missing, and maybe kidnapped." I wait for my comments to register.

The voice on the other end continues to speak in a low tone. "Hey hot stuff. I'm sure the old screw is fine. But in case something has happened to him, I'll send my best tracker to you. If you find him before Luis gets there, feel free to put him to work." He disconnects and I sit down heavily in the closest chair.

I pull one of the laptops over and shake the mouse to bring it to life. I send out an alarm to all our team leaders and their seconds. They should start to appear in the garage over the next few hours. I send information to our teams overseas so they're in the loop in case we need to call in reinforcements. This has the added benefit of getting a call from Eric and Kenny. After the death of one of our own and a close friend to them both, they decided a change of scenery was needed.

I called Aiden in our London office, and he was grateful to have them. I assured them both things were under control. I also made sure to thank Kenny for convincing his brother Kenzie to join us. They are identical in all the ways which matter. When I finish talking to them, I remember to call down to Hector so his staff will not be too surprised when the parade starts showing up. I also asked him to send the team leaders up to the boardroom.

CYNICAL PLAY

I sat back in my chair and start to think about the video. I know the poor screaming bastard we heard could be anyone. Hell, it could be one of his own people he blames for us taking out his kid. Either way, I need to make sure our people are all accounted for, and of course, I need to find Jack!

As the leaders and their seconds start to arrive, the building quickly fills up with large men of all shapes, sizes, and colors. As soon as they get to the building, Hector sends the team leaders up to the boardroom. As soon as the first ones enter, we get to work confirming the location of each of their team members. As time passes, I look around the room and note seven individual teams have completed their verifications. I send them out to search for Jack as the rest of the teams complete their confirmations. Once they're done, I will send them to reinforce the security for our buildings.

I hear yelling out in the hallway, which doesn't happen inside our walls and I rise from the chair to see what's going on. As I get closer to the door, I can hear the voices in the entryway.

"Look, she sent for me and I'm not waiting for a formal introduction. What the hell is this, Buckingham Palace?"

The next thing I know, the doors push completely open, and Luis is taking up the entire doorway. He is six feet, ten inches and looks like a polar bear who's put on a human skin suit. All long hair and tan skin. The man's a remarkable sight.

I see there is more than one of our men behind him. I look around him and hold up my hand to stop their progress. "Gentlemen, we're good here." They stop their forward progress and give Luis a last look. They shut the boardroom doors without a word.

I jumped to hug him. "You know you're terrifying, right? Not to mention they thought you escaped from a zoo."

"How you doin' darlin'? I hear the old screw got himself lost." He squeezes me and drops me back on my feet.

"Luis, I have no idea where he is. No cards, no phones and I've had guys out looking for him since we figured out, he was missing. I'm starting to think he may have been kidnapped. To be fair, given the shit I pulled, it wouldn't surprise me if he kept driving until the truck ran out of gas."

Luis puts his frying pan sized hands, directly on my shoulders and looks down into my eyes. "We both know if Jack were kidnapped, your guys would have found multiple bodies by now. He wouldn't have gone down without taking a few of the fuckers with him. On the other hand, you may be right. If he ran out of gas somewhere he may have decided to live there."

I nodded and motioned for him to sit down. "I agree, but you know as well as I do, it can take a couple of hours for bodies to turn up in this town. Especially if they go old school and do their business in the desert. But if he has run out on me, then maybe we must wait until he gets bored and comes back."

He shrugs in acknowledgment and takes this opportunity to flop on the overstuffed leather couch.

"Luis, can you see the screens from your lounging position?"

CYNICAL PLAY

"Yeah, babe, I'm pretty sure ET can see these damn screens." He waves his hand toward the large wall of monitors.

I queue up the second message and play it for him all the way through. He sits up and makes a motion with his hand for me to play it again. I whistle, he gets up and puts up his large hand. I throw him the remote and he catches it and moves towards the screens. He stands in front of them with his eyes closed. After about five minutes he extends his arm. I've been waiting nearby and have the headphones I knew he'd want, ready to go. I hand them to him already synchronized to the monitors. I go back to the laptop to check in with Kenzie and Cane.

CHAPTER 7

Cane answers on the first ring and I tell him there's been no word yet, but the tracker I called is in the building and already doing his thing. He tells me he's heading into Red Rock Canyon to look for any sign of Jack and he'll call me with any news.

Kenzie was next on my call list, but Luis took off the headphones and has a look on his face which doesn't say good news.

"What?" I ask as calmly as I can under the circumstances.

Luis cracks his neck, and it sounds like a tree falling in the forest. "Well, I'm almost sure the person screaming isn't Jack. The poor bastard in the video is suffering though."

I can't hide the relief, and I know Luis doesn't judge me for it.

Luis starts walking towards me. "Look babe, I'm not saying one hundred percent it's not him, but my gut's telling me it's not. So, this means I need to get to work. Where was the last place you saw the old fucker?"

"The plane when we landed. He took one of the trucks sent to get us and drove off. In all fairness I pissed him off. Let me call the IT people and see if they've located the damn truck."

I hit the intercom button for the IT team. "Benji?"

CYNICAL PLAY

"Yes Boss?" He sounded a bit frazzled.

"Did you find the truck Jack took off in?"

"Yes and no."

"Benji!" I yell into the intercom.

"Boss, wait. I found the part of the truck with the tracker, but the truck is not in one piece anymore. The last place the GPS downloaded, before it shut down, is the private strip club Jack frequents."

"So, you're telling me he went to a boob club and the truck was stolen and has since been stripped down for parts?" I try to keep calm as I ask my question.

"Yes, Boss," is Benji's quick response.

"Send me the location of the tracker, NOW!"

"Already sent," Benji said.

I disconnected the call and looked at Luis. "So apparently you should start at the booby club." I tell him I will forward him the information from Benji as well as the name of the club. He leaves without a word.

I reach out to the phone on the table to call Kenzie and my phone starts to ring. The caller I.D. says Joker2, and I hit the speaker button. "Did you find him?"

"No, boss, but I have some more places to look. Have we heard any updates from the hospitals and the like?" He asks.

"Yeah, we have people posted at each one checking on any current and incoming John Doe's dead or alive. They are calling every thirty minutes whether they have news or not. The latest info we have is the truck he took has been stolen and stripped down. Luis is on his way to the private club Jack goes to. It's the last place the truck was all in one piece," I tell him, tapping my finger on the table.

"What a jack ass, it was a great truck. Boss, we'll find him."

"Keep looking." I push back in my chair, fold my arms on the table and put my head down. I really have run out of places to look for him. At this point, with all the effort and costs we're expending to find him, perhaps if he were dead, it would keep me from killing him.

While I wait for word from someone, I keep working on the sounds and photos from the messages Benji is regularly sending me. I know I've lost track of time because when the phone finally rings, I notice the lights on my desk phone are bright in the now dark room. The sun has obviously set. My contacts are dry, and my vision is less than clear. I can't see the caller ID, but I push the answer button anyway.

"Yeah" I say with a bit of a scratch to my voice.

I hear Kenzie laughing and he's excited. "Boss, I found the old bastard. I found him."

"Let me talk to him" I say with both excitement and a bit of annoyance rushing to my voice.

"Wait boss there's a bit of a hitch in our gitty-up."

"What do you mean? Where are you?" I asked, frustrated.

"I'm downtown… Because he's in jail. The bond is high. Boss, I'm talking five figures high. One of the intake girls recognized him from a bar he and I go to. She called me when she came on shift."

"I'm on my way."

"No worries boss, I'll be here."

I hang up, take out my cell and call Cane with the latest information as I push open the stairwell door. I fly down the stairs as fast as I can without breaking something. When I got to the garage, I notice my parking space is empty. I yelled for Hector. He hurries from his office and joins me.

"Alex?" he asks, confused.

"Hector, where's my truck?" I ask pointing to my empty space.

"I'm having the tires changed. What's going on?"

"Jack has been found; I need to go!" I grabbed his hand trying to convey my urgency.

"I can have them throw everything on real fast, but it would be easier if you took one of the other cars. The Merc is ready and up front, the keys are in it."

"Crap." I say, mostly to myself. I know it's easy to take another car, but for no reason, my brain tells me I need to go in my truck.

Then an unfamiliar deep voice enters the conversation. "Excuse me, Boss? I can take you wherever you need to go. Our truck is right here and maybe a little less conspicuous than a Mercedes."

I turn to find a Polynesian beast of a man standing not too far away from us. He must be at least six foot, six inches with long black hair and ice blue eyes. He also has the best facial hair in the history of humanity. I'm trying to go through my mental rolodex, but nothing is registering. "And you would be?" I ask as my brain kicks in.

"Sorry, my name is Lowe. I came in with Josh."

"Let's go." I say without thinking any more about where my truck is.

He beeps his truck, so I know where I'm going. I use the automatic sidestep to get into the passenger seat. Before I can buckle up, he's already put the truck in drive, and we're racing out of the garage. I lean forward and quickly enter the address for the county lock-up in the truck's GPS. He makes quick work of traffic and best of all doesn't force any conversation.

The county jail is downtown, and as with any downtown area, there are too many damn one-way streets. It's a complete pain in the ass. It seems no matter where you want to go; you must always make a fucking square around the block to get there. I point over to a parking lot where the police cars are all parked, and I tell Lowe to pull in. He doesn't even question the instructions. He pulls up to the guard gate like this is something he does every day. I wave at the officer in the booth. He recognizes me and opens the gate as he waves back. Out of the corner of my eye I can see a small smile spread across Lowe's face.

As he pulls up to the building, he doesn't get a chance to stop the truck before I'm sliding down and hitting the intake door at pace. Between the outside door and the entrance there's a small containment space. The desk clerk must buzz you in. This keeps the crazy people out or in, it depends on the desk clerk. I push the buzzer to get someone's attention. As the buzzer goes off, I can feel Lowe standing behind me. The clerk's voice comes over the intercom. "Please place your ID on the screen to your right." I pull mine out of my pocket and Lowe pulls his out of his shirt pocket. We wait for what seems like forever then we hear the door unlocked. I pulled it open and looked around for Kenzie.

"Boss." I heard his voice to the left of where we entered. Kenzie is standing by the door leading to the release area.

CYNICAL PLAY

"You confirmed it's him?" I ask him without any pleasantries.

"Yep, the woman who called me was nice enough to give me a copy of his booking photo." He pulls the photo out of his back pocket, and much to my chagrin, it's Jack. He looks rough but it's him. "Boss, what's with the Polynesian Yeti? Wait do the islands have Yeti's?"

It takes me a minute to comprehend what he's said. I make introductions which is all my brain can manage. "Kenzie, this is Lowe. Lowe, this is Kenzie. He drove since Hector decided to change the tires on my truck. Lowe works the Pacific with Josh."

Kenzie sticks his hand out. He and Lowe do one of those bro handshake hugs. I leave them and ask the desk sergeant how long it will take to process Jack out. He tells me, not long, but he lets me know exactly how high Jack's bail is. He's also nice enough to hand me the arrest paperwork, at least I will get to see what I'm paying for.

I take it and hand it to Kenzie since my brain isn't comprehending much. "What are the charges?"

Kenzie skims through it quickly, "Basically, drunk, disorderly and multiple assaults."

I shake my head and pinch the bridge of my nose.

"It's all it says boss." Kenzie rolls the report up and puts it in his pocket.

I shake my head and walk to the bail windows. I get in line to wait for a cashier to be available. It feels like forever until I step forward and give the cashier the case number. The woman behind the glass tells me it's going to be $50,000. I turned and looked at Kenzie. Now he's the one shaking his head. I hand the women my company black card.

She looks at it, slides it through the machine and taps in the amount. It took only twenty seconds for the approval to come back. She shrugs her shoulders. I mean it's Las Vegas; you can't swing a stripper in this town without hitting someone with a no limit black card. The printer finishes and she highlights the parts of the documents where she needs my signature and initials.

She pushes the paperwork through the small opening under the bullet proof glass. I sign an initial everywhere she has marked and push the paperwork back to her. She makes a phone call, gives them a case number and a description. I thanked her and handed the release papers to Kenzie. I also asked him to wait for Jack. Lowe has taken a place against the wall, trying to stay out of the way, but still vigilant. I walk over to him and shove my hands in my pockets to try to remain calm.

"I take it this is not a regular thing?" Lowe asks.

I look up at him, "No, no it's not."

He nods towards the door, and I turn to see an officer escorting Jack out the door holding him by his arm. The officer also has a bag of Jack's belongings in his other hand. Jack looks like he took a good beating. The officer stops at a desk and double checks everything with a clerk. I can only assume they are confirming they have the correct person for release. When the door buzzes open, Kenzie steps forward and hands the officer the release papers. Once the officer confirms everything is in order, he nods at Kenzie. The officer unlocks the cuffs

CYNICAL PLAY

and hands Jack his belongings. Jack signs for them and looks around the room until he sees me.

I look at him and shake my head. I tap Lowe on the arm and motion for the door. We go out to the truck and let Kenzie bring Jack up to speed. I climbed into the passenger seat, starting to seethe. Lowe sits in silence waiting for instructions. As we sat there, I saw a red BMW pulling up to the gate. "I'll be right back" I tell Lowe as I hop down out of the truck. Lowe looks around and I know he's watching as I walk back to the BMW.

Cane lowers the driver's window. "So, it's him?"

"Yeah, it had to have taken several people to give him the beating he got. The bail was fifty large. Multiple counts of legal crap we'll need to deal with later."

Cane points to something behind me. I turn to see Kenzie and Jack exiting the building.

"We'll meet you back at the building."

Cane nods, backs out of the gated area, and drives off.

I take a deep breath and walk back to the truck where Jack is waiting. I'm not sure why he would not ride back with Kenzie but it's his choice. Kenzie is already back in his truck and is pulling up next to us.

"We'll meet you back at the building." I say as Lowe unlocks the back doors on his truck.

"Yes, Boss," is all Kenzie says before heading toward the exit.

I turn to focus on Jack. He looks at me through his one open eye. "Getting in this truck could be hard. My shoulder is in bad shape."

I open the rear door on the cab of the truck, "Mr. Lowe, would you be so kind as to help the felon into the back seat. The ass kicking he took was a bit hard on his old man bits."

Without a word Lowe gets out, walks around the truck, and assists Jack into the back seat.

I wait as patiently as possible while Lowe gets back into the driver's seat. I look over at him and he winks. I smile a bit, but keep facing forward. He puts the truck into gear, exits the parking lot and gets us on the road headed back to our offices. As we made our way through the city, I call Luis and let him know we had found Jack.

I asked him to switch gears and please find the people who took the truck. I also ask him to try and get a line on the people who beat the shit out of Jack. He laughs and confirms the change in assignment.

I hung up and called Benji and asked him to let the team leaders know Jack is with me and all is fine. I also make sure to tell him to relay to them to take twenty-four hours personal time. We should have a plan by then on where we go from here.

When we pulled into the garage Cane and Kenzie were waiting by the elevators. It seems one of them was even nice enough to call the doctor. He was waiting next to them with a gurney and two assistants.

Lowe parks the truck and we both get out. He comes around to the passenger side to help Jack down from the truck and I walk over to Kenzie and Cane. "Cane, you're in charge of Jack for the near future. Let the doctor have a look at him and then make sure he gets our best restricted accommodations."

Cane looked at me only mildly confused, then looked over my shoulder at Jack and then to Kenzie. Jack has the common sense not to say anything.

Kenzie pats Cane on the shoulder. "She means put him in a cell."

CHAPTER 8

Cane looks back at me and I nod in confirmation. The doctor's assistants help Jack onto the gurney and as they push it past us Jack looks up at me. "Is this really necessary Alex?"

I look at him and try not to lose my hold on everything. "Yes, Jack, in fact it is. We dropped a crap load of money to bail you out of jail. You have been missing for more than 24 hours. So yes, it's fucking necessary!" Jack wants to say something else but thinks better of it.

Cane is pushing the button for the elevator like a crazy person trying to get it to arrive faster. When the elevator finally does open, he urges the doc, his assistants, and the gurney onto the elevator. He stands facing us waving as the elevator doors close.

I turn around to the two men who remain. I told Kenzie to show Lowe around and meet me in my office in an hour. Without another word I open the door to the stairs and head up.

When I enter my flat, I find Jacob setting out food. I shut the door and leaned against it. "Jacob, what's with the food?"

"Well miss it's about time you ate something you have to chew. While I'm sure you may not feel like it, you need more than those shakes. I realize it's mixing several chewable ingredients to make them, but you need solid food as well."

I ran both my hands through my hair and pushed away from the door. "Jacob, I'm still nowhere near being able to keep actual food down. Please send all of this down to Jack and Cane. They are on the detention floor."

He's clearly not thrilled with the situation, but he takes it in stride. "It is good you found him," he says on a deep breath. He looks down at the spread of food. "Very well, I will take this downstairs," his voice is tinged with a bit of resignation.

"Jacob, Jack's in a cell. No, we can't talk about it, and no I will not reconsider. One last thing, Jacob, don't even think about letting him out." Jacob acknowledges this is not a request.

He doesn't miss a beat. "Of course, Miss. Your shake is in the fridge. You need to put it on the mixer for a spell to remix it."

I walk past him and pat his arm. "Please call the lawyers. I know Jack's an asshole, but he needs a good defense team. There are people in our city who would love to make an example of him." Jacob only nods. I thank him and he loads the cart back up and leaves the room without another word.

I sit down on the couch, in the quiet, lean my head back and stare at the ceiling. In my mind I don't think I have been sitting there long, but the notification on my watch goes off telling me I've been sitting too long. I shake off the quiet and after a quick trip to the bathroom to make sure I don't look too frazzled; I make a quick stop at the fridge to grab the shake Jacob left for me. I pulse the shake on the blender and toss the mixing top into the sink and head to my office.

I take the back stairs and when I open the panel door, I find Kenzie and Lowe sitting silently in front of my desk. They noticed me and both stood up. I'm making a concerted effort to drink the shake. I motion for them both to sit back down. As I sit, I ask Kenzie if Luis has had any luck finding the people who took the truck and smacked Jack around.

"Last report was he had a few places to check, and he would call you when he found something."

Lowe leans forward in his chair. "Is there something or someone I could be out there helping to find?"

"We are looking for the people who made it necessary for all of you to come and join us in the ass crack of hell. We need to find the people who beat on Jack, and we need to find out if they are in any way linked to the big bad, I'm currently pissing off."

Lowe leans back in the chair and laughs a deep chest laugh reminding me ever so slightly of someone else. It's nice to hear but it cuts right through all the niceties.

"Kenzie have you been down to talk to the old man?"

He doesn't smile. I know he can tell this is not the time for it. "No. Cane was still down with Jack last time I checked in. I'll call him and get a status." He gets up and walks to the other end of the office to make the call.

Lowe continues to sit quietly in the chair with his exceptionally large, tattooed arms crossed over his chest. I make another attempt to drink more of the shake, but it's not going to happen. Lowe uncrosses his arms and extends his hand to me. I look at him and he nods at the shake. I handed it to him and in three gulps, it's gone. "Not bad," is all he says when he hands me back the empty cup. I wink at him as I take it back.

I hear Kenzie wrapping up his conversation. As he walks back to his chair I glance over at Lowe, and he winks back.

"Cane says he's on his way up. Jack told him to tell you when you finish your tantrum, he would be glad to talk to you. Also, he said Jack offered him a considerable sum of cash and no ass kicking if he let him out. Lastly, Jack was concerned you may not be eating."

I leaned back in my chair. "Oh, for fuck's sake." I held up the cup, and wave it at Kenzie, to show it was empty. "Remind me to show Cane so he can go tell old man river I don't need him fucking monitoring my food intake. He should be more fucking concerned with the fact he got his ass kicked by who knows who, and he left us here in the middle of a crises. Oh, and let's not forget we now need to meet with our lawyers to make sure he doesn't go to fucking prison." I hurl the cup across the room. It clatters to the floor as Cane opens the door.

He's nice enough to pick it up and close the door. "I guess you got Jack's message."

"Yes. Please make sure to tell Jack the cup was empty when you picked it up off the floor." I nod towards the area by the door.

Cane, bless his heart, sets the cup on the side table, and replies with only a, "Yes, Boss."

I put my head down on the desk and took a deep breath. All the shit banging around in my head is not for public display. Jack is mad at me and I'm mad at Jack. It would make more sense if we yelled at each other and not the people we counted on. I take another deep breath and sit up in my chair making my best impression of a grown up.

"Cane, please go down and try to talk some sense into Jack. Tell him I'll be down shortly. I need to check in with the team leaders."

Cane merely nods and leaves the office without further discussion.

"Kenzie, if you would please take Lowe and gather all the team leaders, as well as their seconds, in the IT boardroom. We should be able to get through this all-in-one go. Also have Benji send someone down to set up a terminal in Jack's cell so he can be part of this little chat." I get up and Lowe unfolds his bulky frame from the chair.

"On it, Boss." Kenzie says and nods to Lowe. They both turn and make their way out of my office.

As the door shuts, I hear Kenzie thank Lowe for drinking the shake. I exit through the side panel and go back to my flat. I take a seat on the stairs and break down again, but a little less this time.

I pick myself up and take the long way to the IT boardroom so I can make sure I'm all in one piece before I try to speak to everyone. As this room is windowless and soundproof, I have no idea if everyone I wanted here is in place. As I enter, I don't bother to count as there are easily seventy men standing and chatting with each other. Kenzie sees me, nods, and climbs on a nearby workstation. He does a stadium whistle, fingers in the mouth and all. The room falls silent, and everyone turns to look at him. He points toward me. As they catch sight of me, they align themselves into their working pairs.

I waive and ask, "Kenzie, is everyone with us?"

He points to the screens on the workstation next to me before he jumps down. I look down at the screens and I see Jack sitting in his cell smoking. Cane is still with him, and I see him pointing at the camera. Jack's snide remarks come over the speakers and fill the room, "I'm here. I clearly can't fucking be anywhere else."

I roll my eyes and turn back to the group. "Ok gentlemen, who has something to share?" A pair at time step forward and give a short briefing on what, if anything, they have found since arriving in town. They also were kind enough to bring any information they had from wherever they came from. Benji is recording the meeting so we can analyze the reports later if needed.

"Thank you, all of this is extremely useful, and I know Benji will be able to do something with it. We need to find out if the people who beat on Jack are involved with the nightmare we found on the island. We need to keep in mind, these two things may not be related, but we have presumed they are until we know otherwise. If any of you feel someone from your territory would be helpful, please bring them in. No idea is a bad one, if we get the answers we need."

Jack's voice fills the room. "Hey, you know I might be able to assist. They hit me in the face remember!"

I spin around and look at the screen. I see Cane has his hand up. I choose to take this as his intent to remind Jack he's in a cell and should only say things useful to the discussion and a bit less asshole-ish in nature.

When Cane finishes talking to Jack he turns back to the camera and gives the thumbs up. I doubt if it means the situation is under control, but at least I'm sure he has advised Jack to try to keep his comments on the task at hand.

I dismiss the group and ask Benji to forward the recording to me. I know I must go downstairs to have a face to face with Jack. We are never going to be able to finish this if we aren't on the same page.

I take my time going down the stairs. More so I can collect my thoughts and less about being stubborn. As I reach the last step my phone rings. The screen displays Lowe's name. I answer the phone rather than opening the door. "Mr. Lowe, what can I do for you?"

"I think we may have accidentally come across some extremely useful information. I have a cousin who took a job working security for a big shot white guy, who's been throwing around money like he's printing it. It appears the 'end game' is here in Las Vegas. He knows our home office is here, so he calls anytime things link back to this area."

I'm thinking and not talking. "Hey, are you still there?" Lowe asks.

"Yeah, sorry I was trying to think if this could be anything else and to be fair, I don't think it is. If you would please get yourself on whatever job they hired your cousin for, it would be extremely helpful."

"I'm on it," are his parting words before he hangs up.

CYNICAL PLAY

I text Kenzie, asking him to join me before putting my phone away and heading towards the cell where Jack is currently residing.

I don't say anything, simply stand outside the bars and stare at Cane and Jack. I know it's childish, but it serves two purposes. One it pisses Jack off and two, I need to wait for Kenzie.

Kenzie made good time down the stairs and joins me looking at the two men in the cell. I yell down the hallway, "Open five." It takes a heartbeat before the cell door slides open. Kenzie and I walk in and block the opening. I updated the three of them with the information I received from Lowe. It's clear we're all thinking the same thing. I let them know we will need to be ready to go as soon as we have something actionable. I tell Jack he can only leave the cell once he has met with the lawyers. I inform Cane he is the lead, and I let Kenzie know he is second on this one. Finally, I turn and leave the cell without further conversation. I know Jack has stuff to say, but I'm not in the mood to hear it.

I turn toward Cane, "We have someplace to be. Kenzie needs to talk to us about Mr. Hannibal, and we need to resolve the client's concern in the middle of everything else on our plate."

"Christ" Jack says as Cane leaves his cell. "I'm still capable of doing my damn job."

I turned back and look at him. "Jack, you will be doing your damn job from your new accommodations. I mean shit, Jack, what the hell do you think all the equipment is for? It's not like I had it set up so you could watch fucking Sports Center. So why don't you log in and be fucking useful?" I don't wait for a response before waving for Cane to follow as we walk away. Jack doesn't even try to get up. As we walked past the desk I waved at the guard, and he pushed the button to close Jack's cell. I hear the gate close as we reach the elevator.

We reach the room with all the fancy computers and what not. "Okay, we're all here. Kenzie what seems to have you all twisted up with this one?"

"Boss, Mr. Hannibal's people are pressing the issue about dealing only with the top of the food chain for the protection detail. I've exhausted all my nice grown-up words."

I walk over to one of the high-top workstations and drag a stool over in front of the giant monitors. "Cane, please make sure Jack is with us via his new working space." I tap Kenzie on the shoulder. "Please call the ass hat you've been dealing with. Make sure the audio is on the overhead speakers."

Kenzie's joker-style grin breaks across his face. He hands his phone to the tech on duty who places the phone on the syncing pad and Kenzie dials the number. At the same time, I pick up one of the keyboards and ask the tech to make sure what I type is visible on Jack's screen. With a few clicks Jack's face appears on the screen via picture-in-picture.

A pompous voice comes over the sound system. "Boy, you better be calling with the number of your owner because I ain't got time to keep telling you. I only talk to the 'MAN' in charge."

I look over and both Cane and Kenzie are grinning. The poor tech spits his water all over his monitor with the douche-bag's comment. Jack crosses his arms over his chest, and I can see by the look on his face, Jack's starting to understand the position he put us in. I tap the tech on the shoulder and let him know to make sure Jack's mic is unmuted. I type to Jack, "Start the call."

In the gruffest manliest voice, I've ever heard Jack use, he starts to speak. "My man has told me you wish to speak to someone at the 'top of the food chain', to use your words."

"Finally, someone in charge and you sound like a man's man. Good, I need to hire your firm for my client." The change in the guy's attitude is ridiculous and annoying.

"Oh, I'm not in charge. I'm the assistant to the person in charge," is Jack's snarky reply.

"Wait a damn minute..." is the confused reply from the other end of the call.

Jack cuts him off. "Shut the fuck up. I've spoken to the owner of our firm and they're willing to meet with your client."

There's sputtering from the other end of the phone line. "*I* must be with my client at any meetings. He's in danger in case you missed that important detail!" The outrage has returned to the guy's voice.

"Oh, for fuck's sake if *you* could protect him, you wouldn't need *our* firm you clown. Kenzie will call you with a time and location. Have your client there ON TIME! If you are late or try to cause a scene at the meeting, we'll not only refuse to protect your client, but we'll make it known you were unable to secure us as a protection detail. Now, how would it look to the rest of your clients?" Without waiting for a reply, "I'll take your stunned silence as acquiescence." Jack makes the cut off sign to end the call.

The tech shuts the call off, bringing an end to the conversation. Cane and Kenzie are seconds away from wetting themselves because they're laughing so hard. I'm still sitting on the stool with my arms crossed over my chest. I ask the tech to bring Jack up on the screen.

"What? He deserved everything I said," is all Jack has to say when he reappears on the monitors.

"I didn't say a thing. Kenzie when you and chuckles collect yourselves, please set up the meeting."

Kenzie wipes his eyes, "Yes, Boss."

I slide off the stool and tell the three of them I'm going for a drive. "Call if you need me for anything."

I take the stairs down to the garage, passing three employees on the way down. It strikes me as odd, with all the folks in the building right now, but it also makes me happy to know our people are making the choice to take the stairs. When I get to the garage, I'm relieved to see my truck waiting for me. I wave at Hector as I get in without a word. Jack must have told Cane or Kenzie to call ahead. He's not a bad person, but he can be a supreme idiot sometimes. Hector opens the gate for me, and I pull out into the sunlight as Etta James starts to fill the cab of the truck.

CHAPTER 9

I lost track of time driving the strip and up through Red Rock Canyon. The music turns down as my in-cab phone rings and I push the button to answer the call. "Yeah."

Cane's voice echoes into the emptiness of the truck cab. "Hey, Kenzie got the meeting set up. It will be tonight, but we need to fly to Hawaii."

"Excuse me?" I asked, confused.

"Apparently it's as far as he can come this direction during the rugby season."

"Well crap. Call the pilot and ask Jacob to pack me a bag. I'll meet you at the plane in 30 minutes."

"Already on it, see you in 30."

As I make my way towards the airport, I find myself sitting at a red light and bouncing my head off the steering wheel. I take the exit for the private airport and try to remember what was in the folder Jacob gave me. I'm having issues recalling any details.

As I arrive at the airport, I see the guys are already there and the plane appears ready to go. I step down from the truck and one of Hector's men is at the door ready to take it back to the garage. I thanked him and found Cane standing at the bottom of the stairs.

"Jack's on board I presume?"

"Old Man River is already in his seat. He did talk to the attorney and got permission to make the trip if he gets with them on his return so they can deal with the legal mess he's in. Now I think he's telling Kenzie about the time he had to repair a wheel on his wagon to get his handmade clothes to market."

I pause a moment to ask. "Do you think bringing him is a bad idea?"

Cane shakes his head, "No, he needs to be in on this. But I reminded him to clear it with the attorney or we'd both be dead. The good news is, if he continues to act like an ass, we can always drop him in the ocean on the way back."

I nod my head and go up the stairs as Cane follows me on board. He secures the door and lets the pilot know we're ready to leave.

I took my seat and find the case folder there. When I look around the boys are either trying to sleep or have headphones on for TV or gaming. I take a deep breath and open the file. Inside are photos of the client and a brief bio.

James Hannibal is single. He has black hair, dark eyes, and is New Zealand born and raised. The only thought processing is he has a nice beard. I flip through the action photos. The bio says he is six feet, two inches and weighs 230 lbs. He's in amazing shape, quick and given his position and the number on his back, he's the complete package.

The memories of the island are still raw, and they flow through my mind like waves from a tsunami. Unfortunately, the one thing you learn in this line of work is life doesn't care. You need to keep going and deal with your emotions on your own time.

I get into the meat of the file. At least ten photos are of the damage the stalker did to his home. This isn't good. From what I can see the guilty party is a woman. I'm not ruling out a man, but in my experience, women mostly break things they believe are from or belong to another woman. They also tend to focus on the bedroom and bathroom. This has to do with the fact these would be the places you would find items tied to another individual, other than the target.

I pull the pillow from behind me and throw it at Jack. He makes a 'humph' sound as it hits him on the chest. He unbuckles his seat belt and takes the seat on the other side of the shiny wood table.

"You rang?" He hands back my pillow and buckles himself into his new seat.

We don't discuss his prior confinement; we simply get on with the case. "Funny. So, what's your read on this?" I ask him, tapping the folder on the table.

"It screams crazy broad," is his calm response.

I nod in agreement. "It bothers me this person had such easy access to his home. Should we even take this job? We have so many balls in the air right now. I mean we're going to need to overhaul his home along with his life. This may be too intrusive."

Jack is rubbing his beard and clearly thinking. "Well, we won't know how far he's willing to take this until we meet him. This might be his agent's doing. He may not even want our help. What do you think of him?" Jack pauses and I know he is trying to gauge my mental state. "Is this going to be a problem for you?"

I push a handful of action photos of James Hannibal to Jack, and he peruses through the action photos again. I think for a moment before I respond. "You know, he inspired people around the world regarding the game. So, in a way if there had never been a 'him' there would never have been a James Hannibal. If for no other reason, I think we should do what we can."

Jack nods and continues reading the file.

The flight attendant let us know we're 45 minutes from landing. The guys make their trips to the restroom. We are going straight from the airport to the location Kenzie set up for the meeting.

I get up for my turn and Kenzie points at my shirt. I look down and see I missed my pie hole when I was drinking my shake. "Well shit. Where's my bag?"

Kenzie points to the closet near the bathroom. I pat him on the shoulder, and he gives me his damn cheeky evil grin. If he weren't so cute, he'd be terrifying.

I pulled the bag out and put it on the table to find another shirt to wear. Jacob has chosen to go with V-necks and tank tops. Is it too much to ask for a regular shirt? I retrieved my phone from my pocket to check the temperature. It will be a balmy eighty-five degrees. I really hate Jacob is always right on his selection of clothing when he packs my bag. I choose a New Zealand Chiefs singlet. At least it's rugby related, which made me feel better. I go into the bathroom to clean up and change. When I came out the flight attendant tells us we were about ready to land so I take my seat and wait.

The wheels touch down and as we taxi to our parking spot the guys are up getting their gear on. Cane walks up as I rise from my seat. In his hand is a leg holster with my H&K .45 already loaded and ready. "I don't think it will be necessary. You all have things under control."

Cane waits quietly until I give in and put the holster on. He nods and turns to walk off the plane. "Red is dead," are his parting words.

I turn around and realize I'm alone on the plane. I hold my hands in front of me and stretch my arms in every way I can think of, take deep breaths, place my gun in my holster and head for the door.

We all got into the waiting SUV. Kenzie is sitting in the front seat and is clearly friends with the driver. I don't ask where we're going because I trust Kenzie. After about twenty-five minutes we turn off the main road and pass through a guarded gate. Cane taps Kenzie on the shoulder and asks where we are.

"This is private and very heavily patrolled land. It belongs to my friend Moli and his family. One of my sisters is married to one of his cousins. I called him and it's all good. Moli and his sister were picking up the prospective client and his agent. They should already be on site."

Cane nods and sits back in his seat. After another twenty minutes through what I can only describe as well-maintained jungle terrain we pull around the horseshoe driveway in front of a gorgeous house sitting elevated on a cliff edge. Kenzie gets a prize for this one. On the porch I notice a tall well-armed athletic woman with a jet-black hair pulled into a knot and poking through the top of her bucket hat. I would guess she's in her mid to late twenties. I can see a red dyed streak in her hair, a bit of fire in her personality. She takes her job seriously as indicated by the military stance she maintains as she watches our approach. Jack and I remain in the SUV while Cane and Kenzie exit the vehicle.

Cane takes a position outside Jack's door as it's on the side facing away from the house. Kenzie heads into the house to check the interior. I hear Kenzie whistle and Cane opens Jack's door. I get out on my side and make my way to the front of the SUV. The female guard moves to the left as we head into the house. Jack walks in front as Cane and I walked shoulder to shoulder behind him. Kenzie takes up a position right inside the door. Jack nods to the young woman at the door. I do the same as Cane and I enter and close the door behind us. I can see Moli out of the corner of my eye and his family have taken up security positions around the perimeter of the house.

"Good lord is the President coming?" The rat voice of the agent fills the room.

"Miles get a grip. These people flew halfway across the Pacific to meet with us. So don't be yourself for once." James Hannibal rises from the chair and reaches his hand out to Jack. I think he would have tried to shake Kenzie's hand as well, but Kenzie had his weapon out and ready.

"James Hannibal, thank you for coming," he says in a polite tone.

"Jack, and it's not a problem. We understand you can't be too far away from your job at this time of year."

"I've never had to deal with something like this, so I don't even know where to begin." He sounds understandably concerned and motions to the chair for Jack to join him.

The agent decides this is his queue to open his trap. "Well let's start with how many men you are going to send to protect my client and how much this is going to cost us."

Jack looks at the agent and it's hard to tell whether he wants to punch him or shoot him. In any case Jack picks this moment to poke the bear yet again.

Jack turns toward James, "As I told your jack ass agent on the phone, I'm the assistant." Before Jack can finish the agent looks at Cane.

"So, you're the boss. Fine. Now, we can get down to brass tacks. I'm tired of talking to your lackeys." His voice is getting so high I'm worried the local animals are going to get upset. Cane only shakes his head to indicate he's not in charge either.

I notice Mr. Hannibal is looking past Jack and Cane at me. He seems like a decent person, and it looks like he's putting all the pieces together on his own.

Jack snaps his fingers to draw the agent's attention. "Look you wanted to meet the owner, and they have made the trip. If you will shut the hell up, I can introduce you."

The agent perks up at this. No doubt he thinks a three-piece, suit-wearing man is about to come through the door. Someone he feels will be worth his time and his client's money.

"Douche-bag sports agent, this is Alex King, owner of King Consulting. Alex King this is douche-bag sports agent." The poor agent is still looking at the door waiting for it to open.

I walk around Cane and hold my hand out to James Hannibal. "Alex King, nice to meet you."

CYNICAL PLAY

Mr. Hannibal seems a bit taken back but recovers quickly. He extends his hand, "James Hannibal, and it's very nice to meet you."

"Wait a damn minute. I am not entrusting my client to a woman. I wanted to hire your company because your reputation is impeccable, and I was told you're the best in the world. If this affirmative action is a front for the boss, I will not tolerate this charade any longer."

As the agent opens his mouth to continue his rant, I have my H&K out and in his mouth. Cane takes a position in front of Mr. Hannibal. Jack and Kenzie have their weapons pointed at the agent as well. Of course, they are aimed so not to hurt the client or myself.

I lean forward into the agent's personal space. "Miles, is it? I'm Alex King and I own King Consulting. There's no need to keep glancing at the door. There will be no one else joining us. I would also like to tell you we know plenty of sports agents. So, if I decide you will have a tragic accident off the cliff out back, please know Mr. Hannibal will be looked after. Nod if you understand me."

The agent nods and tries to swallow. Given my gun is still in his mouth he mostly drools on his shirt and tie. Kenzie's leans forward and uses the agents tie to dab at the drool. "Well, Boss at least the floor is still dry." He smiles with his crooked smile.

Jack and Cane raised their eyebrows at the comment, and I put my weapon back in its holster. "Jack, if you would please join Mr. Hannibal and myself outback. The sooner we can get to work, the sooner he can get back to his job."

The agent starts to walk out with us, but Kenzie and Cane join shoulder to shoulder to block his progress. He starts to sputter, but Cane shakes his head slightly and points to his mouth. The agent gets the point and takes a seat near the window where he can see us.

The three of us walk out to the edge of the overhang. We can barely see the water, but we can hear it thrashing against the rocks below and we can feel a bit of the spray. I cross my arms and turn to face Mr. Hannibal.

"Mr. Hannibal, how scared are you?" I ask with nothing but business in my voice.

"First, please call me James. Second, I'm scared enough if you tell me I need to get plastic surgery or change countries I might do it."

"Thank you, James, I appreciate your honesty. The good news is I don't think you'll need to do either of those things. However, your home security as well as your personal security will need a complete overhaul. Once this person is stopped, we'll scale back your personal protection. However, I would highly recommend you keep the home upgrades we install."

"My concern is this will draw unwanted attention to me and the team. It's the last thing I want."

I can see his concern is genuine. I turn to look at Jack. He uncrosses his arms and puts his hands in his pockets. "Mr. Hannibal, if I remember your file correctly it said you were single. Is this true?"

"Yes."

CYNICAL PLAY

I run my hands through my hair because I know where Jack is going with this. "Mr. Hannibal, do you like men, women, both?"

I must give him credit; James doesn't miss a beat. "Women."

"OK," Jack nods. "So, Alex, I think we go with a sweetheart set up."

A bit of confusion comes over James' face and I speak before Jack can say something crude. "What he means is you would always have a protection detail, but they would blend into whatever crowd you were in. However, given you are who you are and do what you do, we will need someone much closer to you daily. So, what we do is give you a new… *Girlfriend*. She would be your first line of defense."

James looks at both of us before speaking. "I'm not going to say no, you're the professionals. If this is what you think is best, then it's what I'll do. Will this person show up when needed, or will there be an introduction, so I can get to know them?"

Jack is dying to talk, so I motion for him to go ahead. "Well Mr. Hannibal there's a bit of a hitch in this type of set up."

I roll my eyes because otherwise I may jump off the cliff.

"You see, Alex here is the only woman we have. At least the only one with the skills to keep you safe. So, Mr. Hannibal, I'm pleased to introduce you to your new girlfriend, Alex King."

I punch Jack because I can't help it. "James, I don't currently employ women with the skill set to take on this type of job. However, I think we may have met an even better option to this scenario." Jack looks at me very confused. I turn back to James, "Now if this makes you uncomfortable let me know and we'll figure something else out. The protection would be more obvious, but either way, we will keep you safe."

James shakes his head, "I'll follow whatever your recommendations are."

I nod and put up a finger signaling them both to wait a moment. I walked into the house and to the front screen door.

"Moli?" I ask into the night through the screen door.

The mountain of a man emerges from the ether. "Yes."

"Who is the young woman who was guarding the front door when we drove up?"

He motions for her to step forward. "This is my sister, Kura Tui."

"Hello Kura. I'm Alex King. I have a job I feel you would be very qualified for. Would you be willing to listen to my offer?"

She looks up at her brother and he gives her a slight nod.

"If you're willing to hire me, I would be grateful for the job," Kura answers.

I look at Moli and then back to Kura. "It will mean you have to pretend to be our client's girlfriend. Is this something you'd be comfortable with? Before you answer, know you are not being asked to do anything which will make you uncomfortable. This is a job, a protection job, nothing more." Moli nudges Kura with a snicker as she rolls her eyes not surprised at all by her brother's behavior.

To get us back on track, I continue. "Kura, this is for appearances only." I watch as Kura nods in understanding. "Before we go any further can you provide me a verbal resume of what expertise you bring to the table to protect our client?"

Kura reaches for a medallion on the chain around her neck. She shows me a 75th Ranger Crest insignia hanging from the chain. I'm impressed. "I was an Army Ranger for the past four years. I graduated from West Point and was accepted into Ranger training. A Ranger comes with its own set of mental and physical demands. The Army doesn't reduce physical requirements because you're female, I can guarantee you. The training is extensive and requires Ranger school with combat skills, infantry skills, physical fitness, and water survival. We do patrols in all types of terrain. We are paratroopers, which was always confusing to me. I mean why jump out of a perfectly good airplane."

She smiles and goes on, "The strength an individual needs to manage this training is well beyond the norm. I'm also an Army Sharpshooter. I've added other weapons to my skill set both on the qualification range and while deployed in Afghanistan, Africa, and a few other places I'm sure I wasn't supposed to be. Finally, I've earned black belts in various disciplines." She stops, and I can tell she's trying to decide if she needs to add anything else.

"I resigned my commission two months ago because my mother had cancer, and my family needed me. Her cancer was extremely aggressive, and she has since passed. Over the past month, I've been working and training with Moli's security teams until I figure out what I want to be when I grow up." Again, she's smiling as she stops talking.

"First of all, Kura, thank you for your service. I'd like to offer you a job with King Consulting. Your first job will be protecting our client. Still interested?" I watch a strange look pass over her face.

She takes a breath. "It isn't the greasy one who won't shut up, is it?"

"No, it's the other one." I laugh and open the screen so I can introduce her to the team. She walks through the door, and I hear her whisper to herself, 'Thank goodness'. I smile to myself knowing she will fit in fine.

"Cane, Kenzie I want to introduce you to our newest employee, Kura Tui. She'll be taking over the protection detail for James when he returns home." They both give me a questioning look.

I smile. "No, not alone. She's going to be supported with the original seven-man team I asked Kenzie to organize when we began this case." They both acknowledge my comment and welcome her to the team.

We walk out the back door to where Jack and James are waiting. "James, I want you to meet your personal protection and *girlfriend*, Kura Tui." They shake hands and stand next to each other waiting for guidance.

Jack turns and begins to walk away. "Where are you going? Don't you want you to meet Kura." I asked him.

Jack comes back and shakes her hand. "Welcome, Kura. Good to have you on board."

He turns once again to walk into the house.

"Jack where are you going now?" I ask.

"I'm gonna go shoot the agent." He laughs as he puts his hand on his gun and walks away.

I look back at James with an explanation ready. However, James scratches his beard and says, "I hope he only shoots him in the knee. I rode with him to the airport back home and I don't want to have to drive his giant Cadillac."

I laugh and he motions us towards the door. We get back in the house and take a seat at the large wood table in the dining room to share our strategy with Cane, Kenzie, and the idiot agent. Once the framework for the plan is laid out I ask James for his phone.

I held my hand out to Cane, and he handed me a replica of James' phone. "James we're going to give you a new phone. It's exactly like the one you have but with our GPS and panic software. You'll see no difference, but we will know where you are at any moment, even if you turn it off." I exchange phones with him and Cane pockets his old one so we can destroy it.

My phone dings: I look at it quickly and see it's Lowe. His message reads, *CALL ASAP*. I nod to Jack so he can take over. I wave Kenzie to come with me as I step outside.

CHAPTER 10

I climb into the SUV leaving the door open calling Lowe. "Lowe, you're on speaker."

"Hey, quick. It looks like they are going to hit someone in the VIP suites tomorrow night, Allegiant Stadium. Possible secondary target, no details yet."

"We're in Hawaii, but we'll be there," is all I can say before he hangs up.

I look up at Jack standing next to the SUV and he's already on the phone getting our plane ready to return to Las Vegas. Once done, he makes a second call to ensure we have entry into the event and what the expected capacity will be. Cane is also on the phone asking for weapons to be prepared. Kenzie is the only one looking at me.

"Don't you have someone to call?" I ask.

"Nope. I'm second on this, so I need to wait for Cane to tell me what to do." He points to him and grins at me.

Cane finishes his call, and he nudges Kenzie telling him they must get the gear together as soon as we land. Jack has also wrapped up his phone calls. I look up at Kura and she looks a bit stunned at the details we've put in motion with a few phone calls.

"What do you want me to do?" Kura asks.

"Let's go back and let James know the next steps. Understand you're now his full-time bodyguard. We'll get you a super-secret-squirrel phone like we provided James. I'll send it with your support team," I reply as Kura concurs with a shake of her head.

As we enter the room where James and his agent are waiting, I inform them we need to return to Las Vegas immediately. "While this is not ideal, I can assure you, you are in very capable hands. Kura is the head of your personal protection detail and she'll be returning to New Zealand with you. Her seven-man team will join her within twenty-four hours." James shakes my hand and thanks us for our time.

"Kura, the team being dispatched will determine the upgrades James will need for his home security. They'll also let you know of any changes needed to keep him safe wherever you are. Collaborate with them to resolve any issues you see in their plan." Jack nudges me to let me know we need to go. I look her directly in the eyes, "You're in charge of the team."

She gives a curt nod of her head.

I figure a graduate of West Point should have no problem leading a team. I handed her my black credit card from King Consulting. "Get any supplies you need and charge it to the company. Use this to pay for anything and everything going forward, business, or personal." I see the concern on James' face understanding King Consulting is covering the costs.

"James," I smile, "don't worry you *will* get our bill. Any equipment we deem necessary will be installed by our people. No matter what it is, someone on the team we are sending will be able to take care of it." I handed Kura a business card with a single number on it. "If you need anything, and I mean anything, call this number, and ask for Jack or myself, they'll transfer you without question. Once your team arrives, the phone they give you will have the same number as speed dial '1'."

"No worries," is her quick reply.

"We'll be in touch." I nod to let Jack know I'm ready. As we walked out the door at the edge of the wooded area, I saw a large chipper shredder. I extend my hand towards Cane. "Give me the phone." He hands it to me. "Moli, can I use the chipper right quick?"

Moli follows my eye line and motions for me to follow him. He turns on the machine and I toss the phone in. It bounces around the opening once or twice and then a short grinding sound comes from the machine. I shake Moli's hand leaving behind five hundred dollars and we make our way back to the SUV. Cane is holding my door open, and Kenzie and Jack have already settled in their seats.

I take my seat; Cane shuts the door and makes his way around to the other side. Moli is nice enough to be our driver for the return trip.

Kenzie points out the window, "Up, up and away." Moli laughs as he returns us to the airport.

The only talking in the SUV is Kenzie and Moli. I'm not sure what they are talking about, but it sounded like a good memory. Jack, Cane, and I spent the drive staring out the windows into the darkness.

The flight was uneventful. I hear Jack making calls. Otherwise, everyone tried to sleep. We land and head to our buildings to make sure our teams are ready to go. According to Jack we have full access to Allegiant

CYNICAL PLAY

Stadium. We will enter through the loading dock, and we need to blend in.

We all go to my office, to do a review of our plan one last time as we wait for a call from Lowe. We agree the plan is sound. Jack points at Cane and indicates he needs to make sure his team is ready.

Cane nods and he and Kenzie leave us in the office.

I wait for the door to close before I ask my question. "So, what did the lawyers come up with? I heard you talking to them on the flight back."

Jack shakes his head. "There's a lot of fines and there's talk of probation, but the hope is most of the charges can be pled down or dismissed completely if we can get the complainants to agree to an out of court settlement. Honestly, I'm still trying to remember what happened."

"I know the lawyers will take care of this for you. Their strategy sounds better than jail or prison time to me, so it's worth whatever the cost."

Jack nods in agreement. He's not ready to apologize and to be fair I'm not ready to listen. We talked for another half-hour about the things we needed to put in place to protect James and a thought smacked me in the head.

"Hey, with everything going on I forgot to ask you. Did you put some property up for sale or agree to buy some property and forget to tell me?"

Jack looks genuinely confused. "Not as I can recall, why?"

I look around my desk for the message. I find it at the bottom of the mess on my desk. "I have a message to call Kelly. We need to make sure we circle back to this as soon as we can."

Jack agrees and we continue to wait for word from Lowe.

My cell phone rings again with a video call, and I don't recognize the number. I can't imagine it's Lowe already calling back and he wouldn't use a video call. I make sure I answer the call with the tracking app Benji has put on my phone. I push the answer icon, and I see Lowe's bulky frame fill the screen. I can see his face is bloody and it's very fresh. Next to him on the floor I see another body has way too many holes in it. Given the long hair and the ice blue eyes I'm already assuming it must be his cousin. A narrow-faced man appears on the screen in front of Lowe. He looks like a villain from an old 1920's train robbery movie, thin mustache, and all.

"So, this is the best you have. This infiltrator is all you sent to deal with me. This makes me a bit sad. But truthfully, I'll get you long before you even get close enough to think about getting me. Let this serve as a warning to any of your other little soldiers." With the final sentence he puts a 9mm Glock to Lowe's head and pulls the trigger. The phone drops to the floor and the last image are a boot smashing the phone.

Jack is already out of his seat, and he has hit the alarm on his phone to let anyone in the proximity know to meet armed and, in the garage, ready to go. I'm still stuck in my seat trying to comprehend what I've seen.

Jack being Jack picks up a vase by the door and smashes it on the ground. This does the job and snaps me out of my pause. I'm up and around my desk and following him down the stairs.

CYNICAL PLAY

We smash through the door at the garage level. Cane and Kenzie are already there with at least forty other men. They have every SUV in the garage open and loaded. Some of the men are handing out weapons and other are handing out vests. Boxes of ammo are being opened in the middle of the floor and everyone is stowing extra ammo anywhere they can fit it.

Jack whistles to get everyone's attention and lets them know what we have witnessed. He tells them en route they'll be receiving the photos of both main targets. Anyone who is deemed to be a protective detail is to be taken out. We want the main targets to be alive. Josh is stunned and the rage is clear on his face. I make sure to make eye contact with him so he knows he will be with us. Jack tells them all where we're going and tells them their assignments as they load up in their SUV's and leave the garage.

Once we are the only ones left in the garage, I take my turn to speak.

"Cane you are lead on this. Your responsibility is to find this new player. Kenzie, you're with Cane. Josh, you're with Jack and I as we try to find out if daddy dearest has also made the trip. If we cannot find him or if we find he has not made the trip, then we will fall in as back up to Cane and Kenzie."

Cane and Kenzie take off in one of the remaining SUV's. Josh, Jack, and I took Lowe's truck.

Jack calls ahead and we roll through the gates to the underground area of Allegiant Stadium with only a passing glance from Metro P.D. We parked the truck as close to the exit as possible. As we exited the SUV I reached out to Benji over the earpiece to make sure we still have reception. "Benji you there?"

"Yes, Boss."

"Is Kranston on site?"

"Yes, facial recognition picked him up, he's camped out in S1014 with a large contingent of men and apparently a date."

"Okay, let Cane and Kenzie know where Kranston is." I make a call and put it on the speaker.

"Cane, heads up, daddy dearest is camped out in S1014.

"On our way," Cane responds.

Benji comes back on the air with more intel, "There are twenty-eight seats in the section. There are four seats above the main suite seating. He has at least ten men with him in the suite and there are two outside the door and he must have others roaming near the suite."

"Assignment for the woman in the suite?" Cane asks.

"We don't care about her. I don't want you doing anything to compromise our takedown of Kranston. The woman is to be taken out. Got it."

"On it." Cane cuts the connection.

Benji is back on my earpiece "Boss, the guy with the mustache isn't hiding."

"Do we have a name to go with his ridiculous face?" I ask.

"Not yet, but I'm running all the images we're getting through Interpol and all the databases from Jack's friends, and I've sent it to Eric and Kenny as well."

CYNICAL PLAY

"Benji, what do you mean he's not hiding?" I ask, curious.

Benji's reply is quick and a bit angry "The fucker is looking for cameras and grinning at them each time he finds one."

I thank him and walk over to Jack, he only shakes his head, letting me know he's got nothing new. I tell him what Benji said about the man with the mustache. He looks like he could spit nails. We can all hear as the teams get to their areas and do their initial sweep for the targets. There are people all around us. We are doing our best to not look like mercenaries.

We have about thirty minutes of check-in and Benji chiming in with the targets last known visual. I asked Benji to get into the stadium's security system and tell him he needs to be able to control the entire system from where he is, we can't let a locked door delay us. I also tell him if he needs more help to pull in anyone he needs.

It only takes Benji another ten minutes to get us real time information. At the same time Cane reports he has eyes on their target, he notes Kranston's lady friend is currently asleep or bored. Kenzie reports their location.

"Boss?" Kenzie decides he needs to share his concern for the woman. "I think the woman may already be dead. She must have been Kranston's original target for some reason. She hasn't moved in the ten minutes we've been watching them."

Cane cuts in, "Our target is on the move, repeat our target is on the move."

"Shit, where did he go?" Kenzie asks.

"You two need to stay on Kranston," I respond. "If she's dead, he'll be looking for a quick exit from the stadium."

Cane comes over the radio. "Boss, he's gone. He got up right when I called you. We tried to follow him, but he fucking vanished."

I know Kranston must have had an escape plan. Kenzie is right, the woman is dead. Benji is reporting over the earpiece as the woman slumped to the floor when Kranston stood up and the last bodyguard out the door put her in the cabinet under the sink in the suite.

CHAPTER 11

I leave the garage and head to my flat. I need a shower and down time. We spend the next couple of days taking care of ourselves and documenting the events of the Allegiant Stadium clusterfuck.

I'm sitting at my desk doing my best to clean it off while completing some tasks I've been avoiding. As I'm about to send a pile of papers through the shredder I see a note stuck to the back of the last page. I pulled it off and it is a reminder to call Kelly. I push the autodial for Jack and wait for his answer.

"Yeah?"

"Jack, we need to call Kelly, can you join me in my office please?"

"Shit, yeah, give me five."

I hung up and waited for him. I'm sitting head back and eyes closed when Jack walks in without knocking. He sits down in his usual chair and waits for me to look at him. "We may need to get a damn assistant if things continue at this pace." I tell him without opening my eyes, as I continue to take deep breaths to calm myself down.

Jack laughs, "Like you would let anyone touch your desk."

I open my eyes and lean forward on the desk, "True statement. Shall we call her and see what the hell is going on?"

CYNICAL PLAY

Jack nods and leans forward as I dial the phone.

The phone rang a few times and then a familiar voice answered, "Hey, Kelly, how's it going? I have Jack here with me."

"Hello to both of you. Things are going well and good timing," Kelly says. "I got your order the other day and notification of the wire this morning. I was going to call you later today to check in with you and let you know the order is complete as I put it on a rush as you requested."

There is a longer than normal pause on the line. "Alex, you still there?" Kelly asks.

"Yeah, I'm here. Can you remind me of what property this is?" I quickly grab a pen to write down the information.

"Oh, no worries, it's the vacant lot at 215 and Flamingo and the wire came from a private bank, Randall Financial."

"Great, if you don't mind, please continue with the file, and forward me the email to my secure email account, so I can track down who on my end sent it. Also, I'd like to stop by later today if you have time."

"Sure," Kelly said. "I'm free after four and I'll get the email over to you directly."

"Great, see you at four." I hung up and looked at Jack.

He looks genuinely confused. "I didn't authorize a sale of anything. Last we spoke, there were four options we were thinking about selling or donating."

I leaned back in my chair, "She said she received an email from us *and* a wire from Randall Financial. Do we even have an account with them?"

Jack gets a look on his face which usually means something's not right.

"We need to get our ducks in a row before four. Hopefully, the email she's forwarding will give us something. Get our IT people on this. Let's make sure none of our funds are missing, find out the origin of the email and track the wire."

Jack gets out of the chair without saying a word.

A couple hours later I meet Jack in the garage so we can head over to our meeting with Kelly. As he pulls the SUV out onto the street, he tells me what the IT team found. "So, I asked Stanley to investigate this, and he traced the money and the email to the same person and/or persons. He did his thing and already has a virus wreaking havoc on their systems and has redirected control of their funds to us. I have Cane and Kenzie paying a visit to the private bank."

We arrive at Kelly's office and park at the rear of the building.

I picked up my phone from the center console. "I'll call and let her know we're here." It only took a couple of minutes for her to open the side door for us.

As we enter Kelly's office I motion to Jack. "Kelly, you remember Jack."

Kelly shakes Jack's outstretched hand, and we all take a seat.

"Alex," Kelly smiled. "I would have come to your office; I know how busy you are."

I shake my head, "No worries, given the situation, we thought it would be best to see you. The short of it is, we didn't open an order. We've looked at it from our end and this is someone trying to pull a fast one. Of course, you should follow all your internal protocols and notify the authorities. We're already correcting the matter on our end."

CYNICAL PLAY

Kelly loses a bit of her cheeriness, but immediately starts to make notes for herself so she can make the proper notifications of the fraudulent file. "Alex, I'm not sure what to say."

I wave my hand to stop her from apologizing. "This isn't your fault. Your attention to your customers helped to catch this before it got out of control. I think the takeaway of this entire clusterfuck, is each step in the process matters."

Kelly seems relieved and her usual smile returns to her face.

Jack pulls some folded papers out of his back pocket and hands them to Kelly. "I know how much the numbers mean and we figured we could replace the one bad deal with two good cash deals."

Kelly looks at the papers and sees each of the two new requests were individually worth more than the bad file. "Thank you both, it's very much appreciated. I'll make sure these are taken care of."

Jack and I got up to leave and we thanked her again for calling.

As Jack and I are leaving the building he has a smile on his face.

"What's with the smile?" I asked him.

"It's like they always say about this town. It's not always what you know but *who* you know."

Jack and I don't waste time getting back to the buildings. We stop by Stanley's office when we arrive to let him know he's in charge of two deals we left with Kelly. Without missing a beat, he gets to work and waves at us as he picks up the phone.

Jack tells me he has some things to investigate, so I make my way back to my office to finish cleaning off my desk. As we get back to the tasks at hand, we use every resource available, ethical, and *not* so ethical, to track down and take out as many of dear old dad's assets as we can.

It's not as hard as I thought it would be. Our external teams, across the globe, had been aware of JD Kranston's organization for quite a while. Given he wasn't using the family name and never infringed on their jobs, they ignored the lot of them. However, with the recent events they weren't unhappy with the kill order we put on their team members, taking care not to lose any of our men in the process. We've been relentless as we continue to collect his people and return them in bits or pieces, and sometimes not at all.

There's some good news about this undertaking. When Kenny and Eric heard about Lowe's death, they decided to come home. Lowe had been with our organization for as long as they had. It's good to have them back and to see Kenzie and Kenny together, which is strange, but they're a fantastic team. We hold services for Lowe, his cousin, and their friend. Most importantly we make sure their bodies are sent back to their families, and we take care of all costs. This includes making sure the families get pension payments each month.

It's been a busy couple of days with team leads running their operations from our facility taking out the bad guys, as we get ready to go after the man with the mustache and his remaining associates.

Jack used his contacts in the agency and private contractors to offer a bounty on the man who led the slaughter of our men on my island. It doesn't take long until we get word on his location: London. We will both make sure Josh participates in this takedown. He needs it to close out this mess in his head. The good news is, it's time to take a vacation across the pond.

Before I reached my office, my phone rings and I couldn't imagine who'd be calling as I thought all the team leaders were there. "Yes?"

"This is Kura," she says calmly.

"Hi Kura, what's going on?" I ask.

"I have a situation here. I'm going to need additional manpower." I hear her take a deep breath before she continues. "Our client's team was invited to play in a few exhibitions matches in England, primarily London. I need more manpower to protect him as this will be on a much larger scale. The coach has been brought into the loop at the client's request. He agreed to tell people I'm a new consultant for the team, and my security team has been added to their traveling support team, so we can stay close to James as they travel."

"Not a problem Kura, we already have boots on the ground in England. Do you think whoever this is will show over there?"

"Yes, Ma'am. The team offers travel packages for fans, so the likelihood is better than good. But I have a suspicion she's internal to the team, based on information I've uncovered from James and other team members."

"You believe it's a woman too?"

"Yes, it has jealousy written all over it. The team has a physical therapist who's on their payroll and travels with them everywhere. She also has access to all the players' homes, actual keys so she can get in to treat them as needed. They call her Dr. Jessie. She's nice enough but she's very possessive of James. I did a security check on her, but there were no red flags. She doesn't have a record, but several of Jame's teammates have told me she gets really bitchy when James brings another woman around. They tease him about her constantly. James told me there was nothing there. He's never dated her or shown he wanted any type of relationship, other than professional, with her."

"Sounds like you might be on to something. Have you shared your thoughts with James."

"Yes and no. I've talked to him about the woman in general conversation. He told me, though he didn't think anything about it at the time, Dr. Jessie had come to his house to work on a calf strain, giving him grief. She was giving him a TENS treatment and excused herself to get a drink and use the restroom. But when he went upstairs later to shower, he found the broken glass from a bottle of perfume someone had previously left in his bathroom. He said it had to have been broken in one of the sinks as he found glass chips on the counter and the rest of the bottle in the trash. Since it wasn't even close to the sinks, he thought Jessie had used it and dropped it by accident. He was surprised she never mentioned it to him."

"Okay, we'll do a deep dive into this doctor. When do you have to be in London?"

"Team leaves in three days."

"Ok, I'll call Aiden in London and let him know you'll be coordinating with him. Give me thirty minutes to make my call. Thanks, Kura. If our timing syncs up, we may meet you there as one of our primary targets is in London as well. We should be there before you. If you need anything else, or I get any additional information about your doctor, I'll let you know."

"Later," Kura ends the call.

I call Aiden as I walk to my flat. He laughs and tells me he's proud of me for entering modern times. He expands on his attempt at humor by telling me it'll be nice to work with a woman other than me. I laugh and tell him to sod off. I also call Jack to tell him we need to head to London as soon as we can. I told him Kura and Mr. Hannibal will be there in three days for a few rugby exhibition matches. We may or may not be there at the same time depending on how long it takes us to finish our business. As I enter my office, Cane and Kenzie are waiting for me. I look at them, "You ever been to England?"

"I doubt it, think I would have remembered." Cane responds.

Kenzie shakes his head, "Not on any official record."

I pause at Kenzie's comment and continue. "Well boys we're headed over the pond. Get with Jack and put a plan together. We have a task we need to take care of ourselves, and we need to make sure Kura has the support she needs for Mr. Hannibal as they are headed to London as well."

They get up and leave the office and I head up to my flat where I need sleep and a chance to recharge. I lay on the bed and think back to the last time I was in England. We got a job as private security for a group of highly visible rugby players. This was the first time I encountered Ryan. Of course, it was a few months after the job we became whatever we were, but there are memories there. This should be an interesting trip. I closed my eyes and managed to fall asleep.

TUBE PLATFORM

CHAPTER 12

When Jack and I meet the next morning, we agree we still have our issues with any extraneous members in the Kranston family tree as well as his associates. We decided to have Caleb spearhead this black hole search while we're in England. Given many of us will be making this trip, we need to ensure if they pop their heads up, we're ready to cut them off. Not to mention those of us in England may have to contend with them as well. The father apparently has a long reach and since we killed his oldest son, we could have more than a single front to fight on. Jack reminds me we have a meeting in the boardroom, and we make our way down the hallway without further conversation.

When we push through the doors, everyone appears to have been waiting on us. "Sorry we're late, Jack's knees only have two speeds this morning." Jack pushes me but doesn't comment. I get right to the assignments.

"Caleb, you will be in charge here while we're away. Please make sure you're in constant contact with Jack and Kenzie. No issue is too small. If you have a question, ask. Understand?"

He steps forward and with confidence, "Yes, Ma'am."

"While we're gone, see what you can continue to find out about the Kranston family and how their organization is structured. We need to know if when we take out the hitter and JD Kranston, if this will cause a vacuum or a collapse. Dig deep, we don't want to be surprised down the road."

"I'll let you know what we uncover. Safe travels." Caleb smiles as I know he wishes he were going with us.

Jack and I move around the room speaking to each group of men as required.

"Okay good. I think we've covered everything. Does anyone have any questions?"

I look around at each person to make sure they know this is an actual question and not me trying to end the meeting.

"Boss?" I turned to find the voice coming from Christopher.

"Yes?"

"Given the weapons laws over there are we to carry alternative weapons?"

"Good question. Hector and the man behind the gate will have everything you'll need. We do have, let's call it secret permission to carry over there, but we must remember their laws are vastly different than ours. We need to conduct ourselves in a way so as not to attract attention. You will get a firearm once we arrive, and you'll receive alternative weapons as well. Please do not bring any personal weapons you would normally carry. We want to make sure we don't run the risk of losing something we didn't know we had. Make sense?"

"Yes, Boss!" is the reply I hear in unison from everyone.

"Go get packed, check in with Hector, load into the vehicle Hector designates and we'll see you all on the plane."

Kenzie dismisses them. I follow my own advice and get myself down to the garage. Luckily, I don't have to worry about packing. I have no doubt Jacob will make sure my bags are in the garage ready to go.

I stop and check in with Hector to make sure I don't need anything from him. He's kind enough to point out my bags Jacob sent down and he handed me a pen sized stun gun as well as a blackjack. I put both items in my messenger bag and walked over to Kenzie. "How are we looking?"

He looks at his watch and then back at the line of SUV's. "We're only missing four and they should be down momentarily."

"Is one of them Cane?"

"Yep."

I shake my head and take out my phone to call him. At the same time the elevator door opens and out walks the four men we're waiting for. Cane walks past me with a nod and continues to the truck at the front of the line. I turn to look at Hector and he gives me the thumbs up as the three men who came down with Cane quickly walk to the last SUV in line. Cane already has everything he needs from Hector which makes me curious exactly what's going on with him.

Kenzie and I got into the first truck and my driver honked his horn and our caravan exited the garage.

CYNICAL PLAY

We arrive at the airport and the 737 is ready and waiting for us. The trucks form a single line. Everyone has their assignment, and they get out and begin to move gear from the trucks to the plane. We have a larger ground and flight crew because of the size of the plane. As the trucks are emptied and the drivers confirm nothing was missed, the trucks pull away.

I stopped and talked to the pilot and the lead on the flight crew. In the back of the plane is a suite with an office and sleeping accommodations. The rest of the plane is outfitted with places for people to congregate and there are more than enough full reclining first class seats for everyone.

Some of the guys have never been on this plane before so I will give a few instructions before we get underway. "Okay guys. Go ahead and find a seat. Wherever you sit it's your spot for the duration. Kenzie, Cane, Jack, and I have our spots. You have ten minutes until wheels up, so go ahead and sort yourselves out."

*****

We land at Royal Air Force Northolt airport, about fifteen miles outside London. Aiden has arranged for a customs agent to meet us on the plane and confirm our passports are in order so we can get off the plane and proceed immediately to our destination. Lincoln, Aiden's second in command, is with the agent. He welcomes us to London and informs us the equipment will need to be loaded into the waiting vans. He also lets us know we will be traveling by car to the nearest tube stations, as this is the least conspicuous way for us to reach their facility. Besides our team, Lincoln tells us Aiden has full teams waiting for us on each platform.

As each group is cleared by the customs agent, they exit the plane and start to load the vans. Since I'm not sure daddy dearest isn't aware we're in London, it sounds good to have all the teams in place and traveling in a less than obvious way. Once the plane is empty and each van is loaded, Jack makes sure to assign a couple of guys to ride in each of the vans with our equipment. This decreases our numbers and makes the car rides a bit less crowded. As the cars pull out of the airfield, they each take a different direction to get to their tube station.

We arrive at our assigned station, and we exit the car quickly doing our best not to draw attention to ourselves. Given the size of most of the men, hopefully we look like a traveling rugby team.

Halfway down the stairs, the platform comes into view and there is a train currently loading. I look around and see the team Aiden sent both on the platform and on the train. We start to get on the train and Cane sees something and runs between the doors leaving Kenzie and I a step behind him. There is a crap load of people on the platform, and we are struggling to keep eyes on Cane, let alone exit the train to follow him. Kenzie is trying to get him on the earpiece, and it appears to work. As we hear the connection open, he starts calling out stairwell numbers and arriving train information from the overhead boards. Kenzie switches channels to reach out to Carl to get us some precise coordination.

We can take a short cut along the platform higher up and I can hear Carl typing and cussing as he begins giving us quick fire instructions to catch up to Cane. Carl also lets us know he's trying to get access to the CCTV. I know Aiden can clean up the intrusion later. I remind him to not lock out the locals. We are listening and following his instructions, and I finally hear Kenzie call out he has eyes on him.

They tell me he pushed through the gate to a taped off construction area. He tells me he can see Cane and the person he's chasing. I see Kenzie's back go down a set of stairs on the right back down to the underground. Carl finally tells me he has eyes on everyone. Suddenly I hear Lincoln and Aiden on our earpieces. Aiden is telling me they're coming in from a sewer access point.

Cane has someone cornered on the platform. Carl confirms he sees no exit from his point of view. Aiden and Lincoln verify they can see both men at the end of the platform. Kenzie and I jump down the stairs to the platform when I realize it's the fucker with the mustache. I hear Kenzie curse simultaneously. I know he has made the connection as well and then everything happened at once.

Cane advances and the large air intake behind his target is kicked out from the inside. Cane grabs the mustache man by the arm and the guy swings his opposite arm around and he contacts Cane's ribs. At the same time another man emerges from the air intake with some kind of harness. He quickly attaches a hook, and the mustache guy is snatched back through the air intake. In all the chaos all I can see is a single bright, almost glowing red drop of blood on the ground near Cane's feet.

Everything starts to slow down, and I can see Cane starting to crumple to the ground as Kenzie gets to his side. I see both Lincoln and Aiden climb on to the platform with looks of disbelief on their faces. Aiden is standing in front of me and over his shoulder I can see Lincoln and Kenzie talking with an abundance of emotion. I close my eyes and shake my head, and time seems to re-align; now I'm trying to process everything they're all saying, and I also have Carl in my ear.

I told Carl to send all boots on the ground to our location. I make sure to tell him there is no one chasing the target, but he needs to use all our digital assets to track down the party as they have gone to ground through the air vent. I reach up and click over to the other channel and all I hear is Jack yelling for someone to answer him. In a calmness which surprises me, I tell Jack to stop yelling and to check with Carl for our location. I tell him to get to us as fast as he can, Cane is down.

I don't know what's happened to Cane but the look on Kenzie's face tells me it's not good. I ask Lincoln for an assessment and without a word he picks up Cane in a fireman's carry and starts up the stairs as quickly as possible. I grab Kenzie's collar as he hasn't stood, and he follows the momentum of me walking away and we run up the stairs after Lincoln.

When Lincoln reaches the last set of stairs, I hear Velcro rip, and he hands Aiden a strip of cloth. Turns out his vest now reads "POLICE," and it parts the crowds on the stairs as he yells 'Make a hole'. We follow behind him and surface to the screeching brakes of at least three Mercedes G Wagons. The back of one is already open and Lincoln places Cane in the back. He and Kenzie jump in with him and the car takes off.

Jack emerges from the first vehicle with an angry perplexed look on his face as he watches the car with Cane speed away. He looks at me and Aiden and yells, "What the fuck actually happened here?"

CYNICAL PLAY

Aiden taps me on the shoulder. He points to the G Wagon with no lights and the doors open, he knows my brain is scrambled. I can hear him telling the team exiting the second vehicle to get the police light attached to the remaining cars to prevent them from being towed and to show the correct registration credentials on the cars and to get down to the location on the platform and get into the air intake. He's telling them to use their police credentials to get what they need from the workers in the train station.

Not surprisingly Jack is still yelling. I walk past him and get in the car and Aiden follows. Jack is left yelling to himself on the sidewalk. It takes him a second to realize he's alone on the street. He throws up his hands and gets in the door Aiden left open for him.

The car pulls away from the curb and Jacks starts again with the questions. Aiden relays what we know. Jack continues to ask questions, and Aiden does his best to answer. He also tells the driver to take us to wherever Cane was taken. I'm not speaking now because all I can do is continue to replay the events in my head. We pull up to a very ordinary-looking office building. You would never know there is a full emergency medical facility behind the fancy glass doors and executive designed lobby. A loading dock door rolls up as we pull around the circular drive.

We pull in and before the door is down, we have all exited the still running car and are following Aiden down a set of stairs in the center of the garage. We reach the ground floor, and I look around the cavernous space and see a large puddle of blood and a lot of gauze and Cane's clothes cut to bits in a trail along the floor leading back behind two doors which lead to who knows where. I heard a sound and turned to find the source. I see

Kenzie sitting in a plain blue plastic chair with his head in his hands and his elbows on his knees. I know in my gut Cane is gone.

I motion for Aiden to take Jack through the doors to get the details. I walk to Kenzie, and I stand close enough to nudge him with my knee. He doesn't really react, so I nudge him again. It brings him back to the present. He looks up at me and I can see the rage and pain all over his tear-streaked blood splattered face.

I extend my hand; he takes it and stands up. I would sit down next to him but comforting him right now will make it worse. It's important to use the rage to push us forward. There will be a time to collapse and fall apart later.

Kenzie uses the underside of his shirt to wipe off his face. I tell him it's okay to cry and I remind him we must get all the information we can. Then we can hunt and kill them all. I assure him Carl and Aiden's science teams are working to find the fucker who did this. I put both my hands on his shoulders and looked him in the eyes. I don't say anything; I look at him and wait for him to nod.

I squeezed his shoulders one last time, then I turned and put my arm around his waist, and we walked over together to the large pneumatic doors. I punch the button and as they open the coppery smell of blood, and the pungent smell of antiseptic overcome the space. We push through it and look to either side of the hallway. I see Jack talking to Lincoln and I pull Kenzie with me to the right as the doors seal closed behind us.

Kenzie steps away from me and shakes Jack and Aiden's hands and gives Lincoln one of those man handshake hugs. They walk away together and enter the room a bit further down the hall. I put my hands in my pockets because I've had my fill of human contact for the day.

Jack takes the hint and starts from the beginning. He tells me the guy who was pulled through the vent took his shot and it was a one in a trillion. What we saw looked like an ill planned punch. However, it appears in the guy's hand at about the size of a roll of quarters was a retractable or collapsible ice pick or scalpel type device. It caught Cane between the ribs and punctured his heart. Aiden added his information as provided by the doctors.

Aiden tells me there was no way to save Cane. Not even if we had a surgeon standing next to us on the platform. Cane's death could not have been prevented. I'm nodding and listening to both. Aiden tells me, in a moment of brilliant awareness, and or desperation, Cane managed to scratch a good bit of the piece of shit who got pulled through the air intake. The DNA people have the sample, and we are flying in the best genetic specialist in the country to help us run the guy to ground. Jacks looks at me like he expects me to say something or ask some questions, but I don't say anything. Aiden extends his hand in the direction Kenzie and Lincoln went and I simply follow him without a word while Jack brings up the rear.

We enter a large medical/surgical suite. There's a large puddle of blood on the floor under the pale still body on the table in the center of the room. There's gauze, large absorption towels and medical instruments strewn everywhere. It looks like a great deal of effort was put into trying to save the life of a man whose fate was sealed the moment he ran through those train doors.

My hands are still in my pockets as I carefully make my way through the debris on the floor to the elevated table in the center. On it moderately covered to mid-chest is Cane's lifeless, but strangely at piece body. I turn to Aiden, "We need to get Cane's body ready for transport back to the USA. Can you take care of it? Immediately? I don't want him left down here any longer than necessary."

"Of course," Aiden nods. "We'll take care of it. I'll take you back to our offices and Lincoln will take care of Cane." Aiden replies.

Jack and I turn to leave when Kenzie tells us he's going to stay with Cane until he's taken from the medical facility.

I nodded and we headed back up to the car, I ask Aiden if he's talked to Kura. He says no, but Carl let him know the rugby team will arrive at 10:30 AM the day after tomorrow.

REVENGE

CHAPTER 13

We entered Aiden's facility, and I told them I needed to take a shower and clean up. "Aiden, can we meet up in an hour?"

"Sounds like a plan; Lincoln texted and told me he and Kenzie are headed back. They've taken care of Cane's body. It'll be back in Vegas in around seven hours and at your medical facility shortly after it arrives. Your rooms are set up on the fifth floor." We nod and get on the elevator without another word.

An hour later we meet in Aiden's conference room. The monitors are on, and we can see both Benji and Carl on screen. Kenzie, Lincoln, and Josh are sitting at the table quietly chatting with each other. Jack and I take a seat and Aiden updates us. His team has verified the target's location. Aiden tells us they can be ready to take this guy out in two hours.

Jack starts to stand, and I put my hand on his arm. "Okay, let's slow down a bit. There is no way we are ready to go after him now and we still won't be ready in two hours. We need to plan every single second of this, and we need to think about every scenario, every contingency. So, we're clear, this is not up for discussion." Aiden nods and he's a bit deflated but he understands where Jack and I are coming from.

CYNICAL PLAY

Aiden takes a seat, and we spend the next two hours listening to all the information Benji and Carl have compiled. We find out the target, under a corporation, owns an island of contiguous buildings in London on Savile Row. I can't say I'm surprised, but this will make things a bit less than ideal. From the satellite views we can see construction all around his island. Lucky for us there's a lot of workers for our people to blend in with.

My brain is going a thousand miles an hour. "We need to get people on site. We need to know every feasible option, not to mention we need to know every way in and out of the area. I've only been on Savile Row a handful of times, but if I remember correctly the roads are ridiculously small and it can be a nightmare to navigate."

Lincoln takes this as his cue and begins to place calls to get some of his people on the local work crews. Aiden opens a large two-door cabinet and begins to collect several long leather tubes. He places them on the table in front of Jack, Josh, and Kenzie. Jack unzips the first one and pulls out an incredibly detailed map of the area. Josh and Kenzie begin to open the other tubes as Aiden places them on the table. I'm making notes and writing random thoughts on a pad of legal paper to focus my thoughts.

My phone starts to ring, I look at the screen and see its Kura. "Kura, have you landed?"

"Yes, we are headed to the hotel."

"Do you have an update?"

"Yes, our client is safe and there should not be an issue while we are in country."

I'm trying not to get annoyed. "Kura, let's cut the shit, you're going to need be a lot more damn specific, understand?"

"Yes, boss," and she hangs up.

I look at Jack completely fucking confused. "What the fresh hell is going on? She hung up."

Jack has not replied and my phone rings again. The screen says it's Kura. I do my best not to be annoyed.

I answer the phone on speaker, "Kura?"

"Yes, boss. The client is safe. We are headed to the hotel. I anticipate no issues while we are in the country. The subject of the investigation did not make the flight as she was detained in New Zealand by law enforcement." She continues without pausing for input or questions.

"My team set up cameras in our client's apartment and I planted the seed with her that the client and I were more than friends. I continued to drop hints and played the part I was assigned. I did accelerate the baiting as I saw us leaving the country as an opportunity to separate her from the situation. She took the bait, broke into our client's home, and caused a great deal of damage. The police were called, and the footage was turned over. I made sure she was arrested prior to the team leaving for the airport. Charges are being pressed and I would advise a small team remains in New Zealand until the situation is completely resolved. Report complete," Kura finished.

I look at Jack and he's trying not to laugh, and Kenzie has a grin on his face.

CYNICAL PLAY

"Kura, I agree with your assessment, and you clearly have the situation under control. We will be in London for longer than we thought. We will serve as a third team at the venue should you need us for anything, contact us."

"Yes, Boss and thank you." She ends the call.

Jack starts to laugh, and he can barely catch his breath as he starts to cough. I wait for him to gather himself. "You done?" I asked him.

"Shit no! She's fantastic. It was literally *you* talking to yourself," Jack says over a few coughs.

I look at Kenzie and raise my eyebrows to see if he has a comment. He puts up his hands in surrender but is still grinning.

"Read your stupid maps you bunch of jackasses." I go back to scribbling notes on the legal pad.

We spent the next three weeks planning and filling Aiden's conference room with maps and dioramas. There are Hot Wheels, building plans and utility maps everywhere. At the weekends we are on third team as Kura and her team escort Mr. Hannibal around Europe. To be fair, I assigned us to the third team so we could watch the matches and give our brains a chance to think about something else for a bit. It seemed to work. Each time we returned to London at least one of us had an idea about our Savile Row mission.

Once the matches for Mr. Hannibal and his team were concluded. We made sure Kura, her team, and our client were safely on their plane headed back to New Zealand. I make a quick mental note to speak to Josh when this is over. With Lowe gone, Kura may be a good addition to his team.

An additional two weeks are spent perfecting each detail of what turns out to be a simple plan. We have concluded we are going to have to destroy most of the island the mustache man owns, but we can make it look like it was caused by the nearby underground construction project. Lincoln's people on the road crew have been able to provide us with at least two egress and ingress points which, given the design, is more than I thought we would get, especially in the section of London we were headed to.

As we go through each step of the plan trying to poke or punch holes in it, we eliminate maps and documents no longer needed. Anything with written notes no longer relevant is placed into the nearby fireplace. In the end we end up with three precise plans which are easily exchangeable since we all know first contact can fuck any plan.

It's late and only Jack and I are left in the conference room. "What do you think?" he asks.

"I think it's not going to get any better than this. And I like there are a minimal number of moving parts." I pinch the bridge of my nose.

Jack scratches his beard and points toward the door. We make sure to turn out the lights as we leave the room.

The next morning everyone who will be involved is sent a text to meet in the conference room. Jack, Aiden, and I were already in the room when the others arrived. Aiden makes sure to have Benji, Carl and his tech person Grady on screen and ready as Kenny, Kenzie, Lincoln, and Josh take a lap around the room to have a look at everything. No one says anything as everyone has a chance to take in the room and the plan. After a few more minutes of quiet the questions start to fill the room, and answers are given in rapid fire succession. We spent the rest of the day making changes and adding equipment to the plan.

We have made the decision; we will bring his small island of buildings down with fire and some well-placed explosions to include the death of the mustache man. It is quickly decided that trying to make our exit via the streets is a bad idea. Lincoln's men on the road crew have found us a way out through an abandoned tunnel system, which caused the road work in the first place. They have done enough to delay the job so we can use them before they are back filled and sealed.

"I don't know about the rest of you, but I could use some food." Aiden says as he picks up the phone to call the kitchen. Everyone starts calling out requests for food and about forty-five minutes later carts of food are left at the conference room doors. Kenzie and Kenny are kind enough to fetch the carts but not without taking a delivery fee of bacon they stuff in their mouths.

"Jack, do you see any reason why this shouldn't work?" I must ask, mostly to make myself feel better.

"No," Jack says between bites, "I think even if the entire thing goes to complete shit, we can still kill him and light the building on fire, or duct tape his ass to the wall and bring the entire complex down on top of him."

"Anyone else have any doubts about any parts of this plan?" I ask the room looking at each of them.

There is not one doubt among the group. This makes me feel much better.

"Okay, then let's hear from the tech people. Carl, what do you guys have for us?"

"Boss, we have a name, it's Alû. First, last and only name. He does have multiple aliases, but Alû is his given name. He has a small group of people he works with on a consistent basis. We have them all tracked and marked. There are teams in place to remove them. As best we can tell there will be no vacuum when he is removed from the board. Only a collapse."

Benji takes over. "Boss we would recommend our organization step in and take over anything he may already have in the works. We may be able to prevent some bad shit and take some other less-than-savory players off the board."

I look at Jack and he gives me one of his whatever you wanna' do is OK with me looks. "Benji, we think it's a great idea; please start or continue to put your idea into place. Make sure to send all recommendations to everyone in this room."

"Yes, Boss."

Kenzie takes this pause to ask a question. "Hey guys, so what are the priorities for the removal of any onsite information?"

Grady fields the question. "Anything is useful. Laptops, flash drives, phones and even note pads or anything stored in a fireplace, incinerator burn bags. If you can bring it out, please do. We have managed to hack the main internet service provider, and we have been able to pull bits and pieces from his communications. His security is overly complex, but the messages he's receiving are less than secure. We know there is an incoming phone call from Mr. Kranston at 8:00 PM tomorrow evening. This has been confirmed several times."

There is a moment of silence that I take as agreement. "Okay, we're up. Everyone take whatever you'll need and let's go kill this fucker." I stand and leave without another word.

The seven of us meet in the garage in the morning early before the sun is up. Everyone is in road worker coveralls, including the drivers in case anyone happens to catch a glimpse of us. We have one final run through before we climb into the vans.

Aiden's drivers make quick work of the roads as we wind our way to Alû's island of buildings on Savile Row. Benji and Grady have managed to work their way into the CCTV network without detection. This will provide us with the momentary cover we need to exit the vans. I'm sure somewhere in Alû's mind he felt his home was secure. Unfortunately, he's not going to live long enough to regret his mistake.

While we ride through the city, we pull the face masks out of our pockets and put them in place. We pull up to our drop points and wait for Grady to give us the signal we are clear to exit. Our hard hats are down over our faces, and we make sure to show our backs to the cameras, just in case. Lincoln's crew is ready for us at both drop points and we are out of the vans and down the ladders in less than three minutes.

Jack, Kenzie, and I went into the nearest access point. The others are dropped off at the other end of the street. Again, if someone happens to see us, it makes it look a bit more like actual workers going to work. Aiden and the others made quick time back to us underground. We spent most of the day underground waiting. It's important the street appears undisturbed, and we still have a bit of work to do underground so the sound of daily life above ground will provide us with cover.

Our teams have created an access point at the basement level of the property. The target was kind enough to be trendy. He installed a basement pool, something on trend for London. Add to this, Lincoln's men kept setting off the proximity alarm as they were working, so our target had to turn off some of his security measures. Before quitting time, we get through the thin remaining wall without issue. All things being equal, Alû does have a formidable basement door once we get up the stairs. However, Jack has no issue with the locks on the door and we are inside in no time. Aiden's drivers are gone within seconds and Grady has the on-street CCTV's back online so quickly the locals didn't even have time to react to the glitch. The drivers are now making their way to the pickup points making sure to stop and change inside the van.

We are about three hours early for the phone call. Jack, Aiden, and Kenzie immediately start setting the charges to bring the buildings down. Josh is the only one communicating with Carl, Benji and Grady. We want to keep the chatting and technology footprint minimal, and don't want to accidently blow ourselves up. Lincoln, Kenny, and I each take a floor and start to collect any technology as well as any paper and burn bags we may find.

CYNICAL PLAY

It takes us a little more than ninety minutes to collect anything and everything we feel we need to take with us. The buildings, for their size, are sparce. He had some items he clearly lifted. We make sure to take those items as well, hopefully we can get them back to their original owners or their families. Kenny and Kenzie take everything down to the hole in the basement wall and leave it. We'll collect them at our exit.

Josh whistles to let us know the IT guys have eyes on the target. We all found a place to hide in the flat, Josh, Jack, Kenzie, and I make sure to hide in the office where we found his only computer. I use this small window of time to download his entire hard drive to my backup. I open the drawer in the desk, there is a large sheet of butcher paper showing his attack on my island. Aiden, Kenny, and Lincoln cover the front door, the basement door, and the parking access door. They are to prevent Alû's exit should he somehow get past us.

Benji lets Josh know the target is approaching. Josh gives the whistle signal again and at the same time we can hear the computer ringing with an incoming call. Alû walks in the front door without a care. He doesn't even sense Aiden standing behind the door. He casually walks into the office and sets down his parcels before even glancing at the computer. He takes everything out of his pockets and lays the items on the desk, including his weapon of choice. The computer rings another four times before he finally takes a seat in the chair and answers the call.

"Where the hell have you been?" comes Kranston's angry voice from the computer. "You know damn well I'm hemorrhaging men and money. You said you were going to take care of these people and all you've done is take my money with no results."

Alû takes his time lighting a Turkish cigarette before he answers. "You know as well as I do, they have all gone to ground and are hiding in their fortress of buildings in the states. There's no way I'm getting in there. Besides, there has been no movement from them since I took out one of theirs on the platform. I think they have realized they are out of their depth and moving on to another target." He's smirking as he explains to Krantston again how he killed Cane. He laughs as he relives the events. "The asshole was dead before he hit the ground." Alû stops talking as he realizes Kranston doesn't seem impressed. "I assure you I have a plan and will make my move soon enough," he explains to Kranston.

Kranston cuts him off. "Look you fool, there will be no reason to keep pursuing this if I don't have any people left."

Alû throws his head back and laughs, but before he can open his mouth to speak, Josh emerges from the dark and places the barrel of Lowe's sidearm against his temple. Kenzie comes from the darkness on his left, picks up his weapon of choice and lifts Alû's chin so he can look him in the eyes. Jack comes from the shadows to stand in front of the desk. Alû's eyes only slide over to see Jack.

"The light is green gentlemen. I repeat the light is green." I make sure to keep my tone low and level.

Kenzie uses Alû's own weapon of choice on him. He stabbed him once, like Alû stabbed Cane. Kenzie steps away and Josh shoots him in the head as one of

CYNICAL PLAY

Lincolns' men drives an emergency vehicle down the street masking any sound of the shot.

I'm standing behind Alû but still in shadow. I can see the absolute shock and disbelief on Kranston's face through the blood on the screen.

I move out of the darkness and shove Alû's leaking body off the chair, taking a moment to sit down and wipe off a bit of the screen and look at JD Kranston for a good long minute.

"Mr. Kranston, you're in shock. I'm sure you thought we would give up or get tired. Clearly your associate thought so. At least he *had* thoughts, before we spread them all over this computer. I assure you this will not be over until you join your kid, your useless brother, and this piece of shit in hell." I shut down the video call, pick up the computer and we make our exit.

Jack lets Carl know we're clear. Carl overloads the electrical and the flat catches fire. The fire quickly reaches the charges, and we are two city blocks away when the house explodes. We continue to make our way through the tunnel until Grady lets us know we have reached our exit, where we scramble out of the drainage grate in the park. Waiting nearby are two blacked out Mercedes G Wagons. We go directly to the nearest airport, and we are in the air before the first responders can put out the fire. I know Aiden and Lincoln will collaborate with the local authorities to rebuild the area we destroyed and offer aid in the clean-up. It's what we do.

Once we are airborne Benji calls Jack. The call is quick. I looked at him wanting to know what was said.

"All of Alû's associates have been dealt with. Any technology found at the scenes, on their bodies or where they were residing will make its way back to Vegas."

I nod as I know we still aren't done.

END GAME

CHAPTER 14

The flight back over the pond was quiet. The past few months have been traumatic and chaotic. JD Kranston is to blame as much as any of the choices we've made.

Ryan, Lowe and Cane, no one loss greater than the rest. All will be missed and remembered for what they brought to our lives. We'll be back in Las Vegas in a few hours. Everyone manages to sleep most of the return flight.

We land and our SUVs are waiting for us. The plane is unloaded, and I motion for Kenny and Kenzie to join Jack and I in our SUV. As we pull away from the airport, I tell them, "I have a plan for Kranston, meet us in my office in an hour."

We reach our buildings and once everything is unloaded, everyone scatters. I don't blame them. Each received a text as we pulled away from the airport, letting them know they had been granted two weeks all expenses paid, anywhere they wanted to go, even to a suite at one of the Las Vegas resorts.

I take the stairs despite how tired I am. I know the elevators will be full and I need some time alone. My flat is cool and clean. The travel isn't hard, given our resources, but there's nothing better than showering in your own bathroom. I stand in the shower for longer than usual trying to prolong keeping my brain empty. When I notice my fingers starting to prune, I turn off the water and get dressed.

I expect to see Jacob when I leave my bedroom. I make a mental note to ask Jack if he knows where he is. I get a Pellegrino from the fridge and make my way to my office. I take a seat at my desk, turn on some Ashley McBryde and wait for the others. Jack enters without knocking, Kenzie and Kenny are two steps behind him.

I motion to the chairs in front of my desk, "Everyone take a seat, we need to discuss the next few weeks. First, Josh has gone back to his home to assist Lowe's family with his celebration of life. Second, Jack, where is Jacob?"

"He said he had few things to look into for Cane's arrangements and I asked him to check on some other things for me. Oh, and he was going to handle the removal of the idiot who originally forwarded the messages from Kranston to us. Said he knew exactly who could take care of it for us." Jack motions for me to continue.

"Okay, as we talked about on the plane, Jack, will remain here to take care of his legal mess and to make sure Cane gets to his final resting place, which is clearly being taken care of. As he had no family to speak of, he would be interred in accordance with his wishes in the memory wall. Also, you will coordinate with the contractors and make sure all Kranston's eggs are in one basket. We will only get one shot at this."

Jack nods, "So, what's the next step?"

"Kenzie, Kenny, and I will depart first thing in the morning. We'll be moving off the grid for a bit. Cash only, basic burner phones and we'll be living in a large RV. This job will take as long as it takes. We have pieces in motion and Jack will set the rest in motion shortly. We will have all the food and water we'll need for at least four weeks. If it takes longer, we'll need to fend for ourselves."

Kenzie and Kenny both have the joker grin on their faces; it's both comforting and unsettling. "Kenzie you're on weapons and tactical. Bring anything we may need. There will be steel, ground cover and water to contend with. Kenny you will be onsite tech as well as logistics, please consider the same items as your brother. Okay, see you two in the morning, 7:00 AM in the garage."

Jack is helping to load the RV when I get down to the garage. He laughs, "I expected you ten minutes ago." I threw my lumpy bag at him. "Jacob is on some secret missions, and I had to pack my own bag."

He laughs again, "Well it explains why it looks like you're smuggling melons." I punch him and look inside the RV. Everything is as requested. I turn as the elevator doors open. Kenny and Kenzie exit in step, and I notice their bags are perfectly packed. We loaded into the RV with Kenny driving.

*****

We find a truck stop with spaces for RV's and make camp. Kenny unhitches the small Toyota truck we've been towing behind the RV. All three of us got in and we hit the road. At about ten miles from the property in question we pull over to get our bearings.

After three hours of observing we headed back to the RV. We spend the first three days using a drone and satellite images to learn as much as possible about JD Kranston's property as we can. We see an Olympic size pool at the edge of the property, I know this will be the end game.

As the days progress we pay a few homeless people to walk the perimeter of the property with well-hidden GoPro's. Into the second week Kenzie spends hours on his belly crawling his way onto the property to set up cameras. The video captured by the homeless people before they were strongly encouraged to move on by Kranston's security shows us there are at least four dogs running loose on the grounds. We spent several days making friends with the dogs, working on creating a removable space in the steel fence and digging an area under the same fence area. This will make things much easier when the time comes.

*****

At the start of our third week, I received a text on my current burner phone. It's a photo of the tile in Kranston's swimming pool with the manufacturers name and the color. Along with the photo are the words. "Miss, thought this would be helpful." Now I don't know how Jacob knew any of this or how he got this information, but it completes my plan.

I turn on the computer and link up with the secure satellite. I then upload the color I need and wait for a response. Tina lets me know she can have something to me in less than a day. She also tells me she has the rest of the equipment I asked for and it will not be an issue to make everything the same color. All three of us read for an hour or so then fall asleep in our separate spaces. Later, I receive a text from a blocked number. It's the number '7'.

I get up and make sure I have a secure link before I open the message. The message is from Tina giving me GPS information for the drop spot with a time and instructions. I log off and walk past Kenzie and Kenny's bunks tapping them on the shoulders as I nod to the door. They get up, put on their boots and Kenny grabs the keys to the truck. We drive an hour until we reach the designated spot. Kenny pulls over and I get out.

Kenzie raises the hood to make it look like another old truck broken down on the side of the road. There's a freeway phone box nearby and as Tina said there is an envelope taped to the back. I open the envelope and follow the instructions inside. Over a short fence and ten minutes later I had the parcel, and headed back to the truck. As I make my way back over the fence I yell at Kenzie, "Oy."

He looks in my direction, nods and closes the hood of the truck.

We get back in the truck and make the drive back to the RV. I immediately unpacked the package. Inside is a full wet suit, snorkel with a mask, a shallow dive oxygen tank and an underwater body camera.

CYNICAL PLAY

I hold up the wetsuit. "Jacob got the color info of the pool and Tina made this."

Kenny shakes his head, "Sweet."

"Damn!" Kenzie says, "He'll never fuckin' know."

Kenny whistles softly at me and when I look up and he's holding up two meal choices. I point at the veggie rice steam bag. He proceeds with our meals while I pack the bag for later. I make sure to wrap everything I received in the bag I've been dragging behind me the last few nights. We finish dinner in silence and get a couple of hours sleep.

*****

At midnight all our watch alarms begin to sound. We get up, put on the same black clothes we have been wearing since we started this. We don't want to introduce any new scents to the dogs. We make the drive to the designated spot for the last time. As we did the previous nights, we make sure to take a different path than any previous night as we approach the property. We reach the fence and wait. It takes about an hour until we start to hear the expected sounds.

Kenny starts the timer on his watch, I start to change into the wet suit and Kenzie is on lookout. The man servant is out at the pool making sure it's clean. He lays out a robe, slippers and turns out the lights inside the pool. Not something he's done the last few nights, but it's helpful. At one point we pondered why this guy swam so late at night, but in the end, we decided it didn't matter.

I tap Kenny on the shoulder, and he removes the rock he has placed at the base of the fence. We spent a good amount of time digging the hole to make sure I could easily slide under without getting stuck. He lays down the tarp, pours baby oil on it and I slide under the fence and Kenzie places the weighted belt on the other side for me. I put on the weight belt and plank walk towards the pool. As I reach the edge of the grass the dogs come running around the corner. But they don't even bother with me. They go right to the opening at the bottom of the fence to visit Kenzie and Kenny. They, of course, have treats for them.

I finished my progress to the pool, quickly sliding into the water, making as few ripples as possible. I wet the mask and put the mouthpiece attached to the small tank in and let the weight belt take me down. I make sure to pull over the veil attachment to cover my face to complete the blending in with the pool surface.

Forty-five minutes later the lights around and in the pool came on. He's right on time. Impulse control is paramount in this kind of situation. Nothing worse than letting the rage over power the planning. I watch from below as he takes his first two laps, and I wait for him to follow his routine. He doesn't disappoint. He's now only inches from me. As he partially lifts his head out of the water and opens his mouth to take a deep breath I shove a piece of medical tubing into his mouth.

When his eyes flash open, I spray the fast-acting lidocaine mixed with succinylcholine through the tube. I pull off my mask and watch recognition, disbelief, and fear flash through his eyes. I continued to hold the tube in his mouth letting the water flow in. I flip him over and use my weight to drive him to the bottom of the pool. I start to see his body giving itself over to the water. When his eyes are finally bulging, I remove the tube, and take off the weight belt and secure it around his waist. I slowly make my way to the surface. I reach the edge and as I break the surface, I hear Kenzie whistle letting me know the coast is clear.

I stand up and walk to the fence and slide underneath. While I was on the other side of the fence Kenny and Kenzie were busy at work. I get out of the wet suit and back into my original clothes. I notice the dogs are now on the other side of the fence sitting quietly. I look at Kenzie and he shrugs. Kenny rolls up everything and puts it back in his pack. As we all walk away Kenzie flicks matches every few feet. We continued making our way back to the Toyota without saying a word. The dogs follow us and jump into the back of the truck without instruction.

We get about a mile down the road when Kenny pulls over to the side to let the emergency vehicles headed in the opposite direction go past us on the two-lane road. We look back together through the rear window and see an enormous wall of fire at the perimeter of the property and then the explosions start. We waited about ten minutes and pulled out into traffic. Back at the truck stop we hitched up the Toyota to the RV and headed back to Las Vegas.

"We should be back in time for breakfast. Four hours out, right." I ask Kenzie.

"Give or take. Breakfast sounds good to me; it'll be nice to eat something which hasn't been nuked?" Kenny laughs.

As we got on the freeway Kenzie turned to me. "You know my favorite part of footy is the cynical play. You know it'll get you sent to the bin, but it also serves as a warning." I consider what he's said, and I smile in agreement.

THE END

About the Author

L.M. Causey resides in Las Vegas and is a graduate of UNLV with a B.A. In Criminal Justice. Being raised in a multi-generational military family, along with travel both local, across the U.S. and abroad have inspired her stories.

She is a fan of New Zealand Rugby, the All Blacks, and was in London in 2015 to watch her favorite team win the World Cup. Her significant other has introduced her to other favorites: *Family Guy, Bob's Burgers* and *American Dad*.

Music is a big part of her writing process, popular bands being the *Kenny Wayne Shepherd Band* and *Halestorm*.

And yes, she does own an HK .45.

Contact the author at:
Instagram: lisalasvegas777
Twitter: @LisaLasVegas777
Facebook: L.M. Causey

Also from L. M. Causey

Alexandria Anastasia King, aka Alex, is a woman with new-found wealth, freedom and a mission in life. A bad marriage and the murder of a friend put her on the path to make things right in the world...in her own, unique, way. With friend and mentor Jack Sterling, ex-intelligence operative, they established KING Consulting. It's an enterprise she describes as, 'a businesspeople tend not to talk about, but everybody wishes they had on speed dial'. Under Jack's guidance she learns hand-to-hand combat, firearms and knife skills, preferring a Heckler and Koch .45 and KA-BAR combat knife. She and Jack recruit their selected cadre of team members and take the jobs other agencies defer. Where Alex and her team go, trouble is never far behind, from the sewers and hotels of Las Vegas to the tropical isles.

Available as an e-Book, print and audio book, narrated by Kellie Kamryn.